The OTHERLANDS

STEVE SKINLEY

Crumps Barn Studio

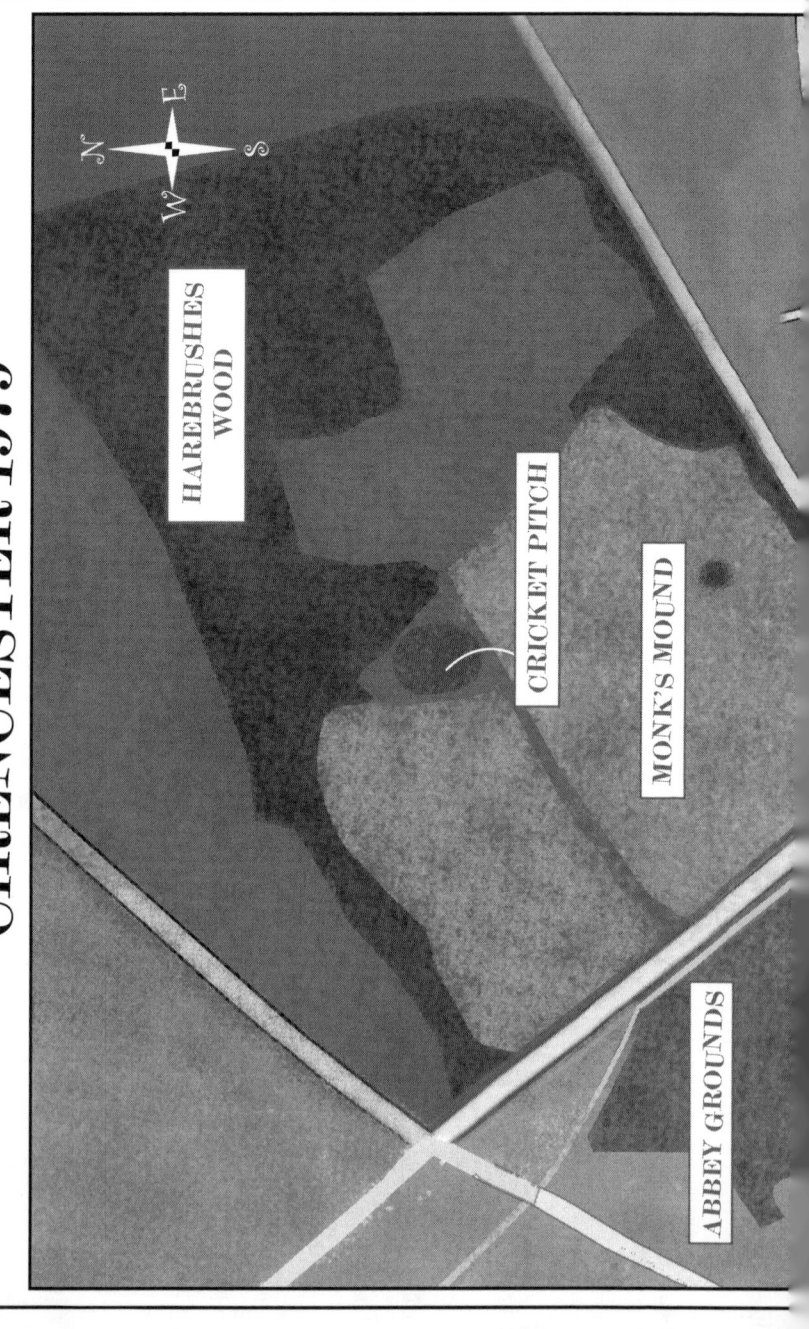

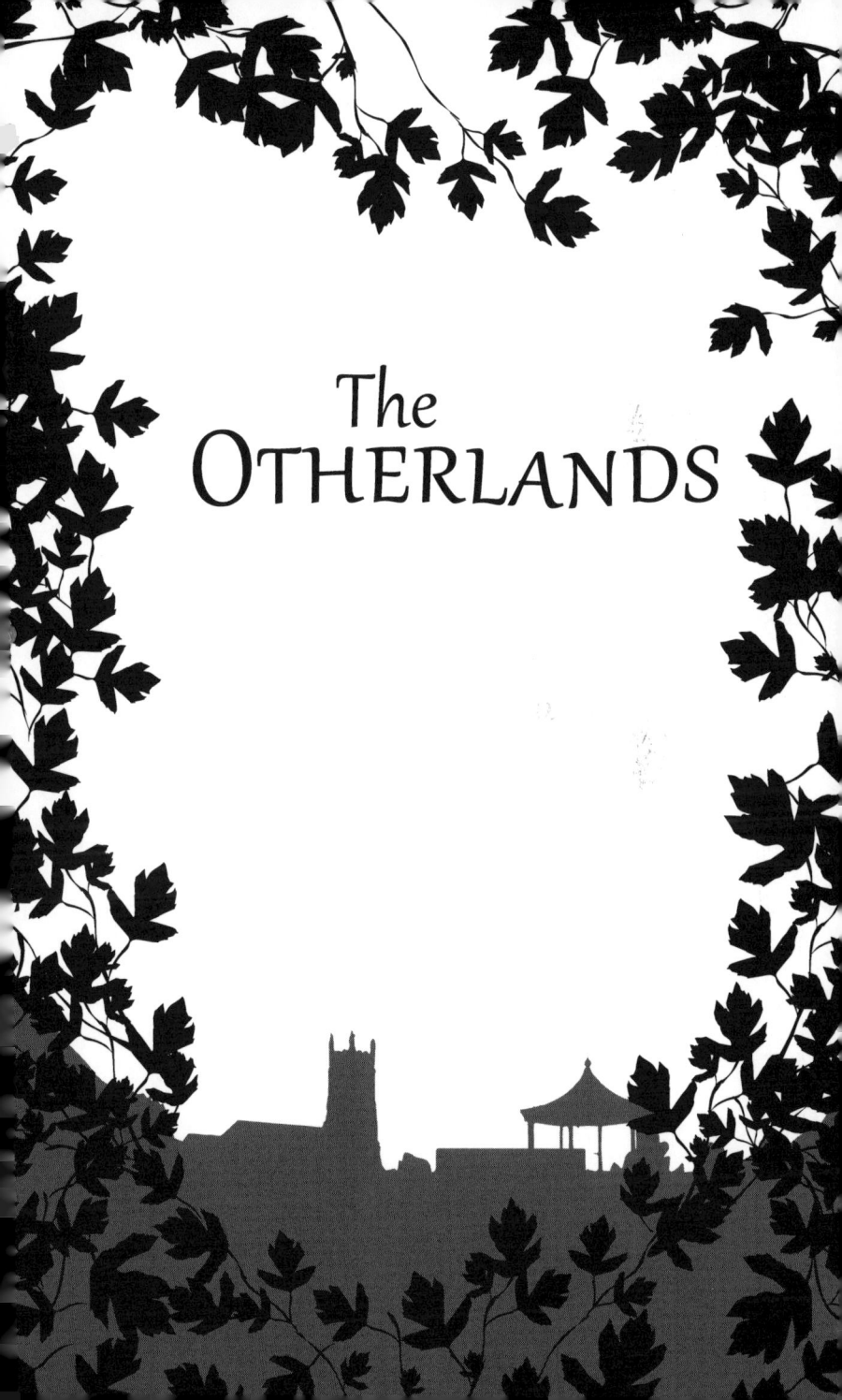
The OTHERLANDS

*For my family and friends and
the good folk of Cirencester*

Crumps Barn Studio
No.2 The Waterloo, Cirencester GL7 2PZ
www.crumpsbarnstudio.co.uk

Copyright © Steve Skinley 2024
Maps copyright © Steve Skinley 2024
First published 2023
This edition 2024

The right of Steve Skinley to be identified as the author of this work has been asserted in accordance with the Copyright, Designs and Patents Act 1988.

All rights reserved. No part of this publication may be reproduced, stored in a retrieval system, or transmitted in any form or by any means, electronic, mechanical, photocopying, recording or otherwise, without the prior permission of the copyright owner.

Cover design by Lorna Gray

All our books are printed on responsibly sourced paper from managed woodlands. Printed in the UK by CMP, Poole.

ISBN 978-1-915067-31-9

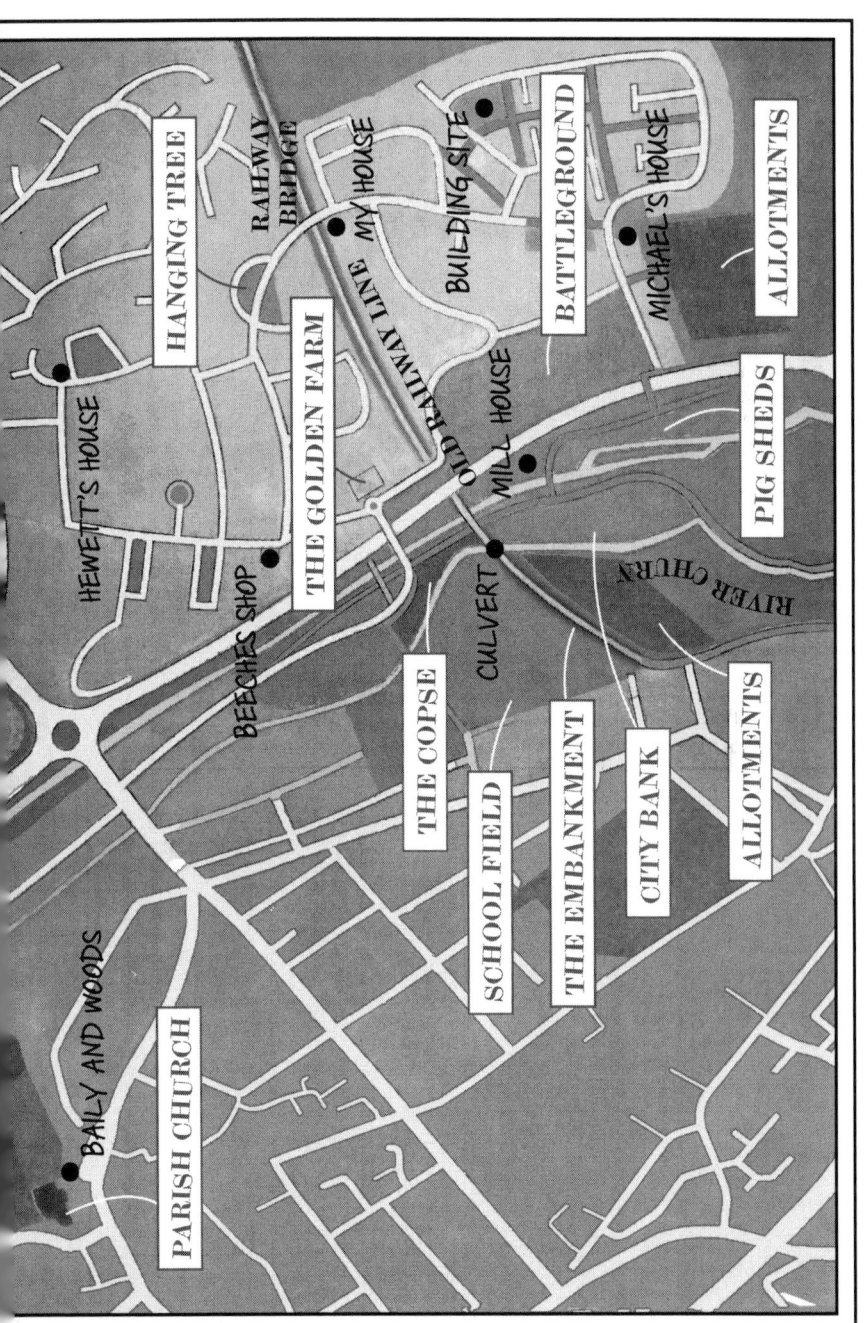

THE OTHERLANDS

N E S W

HANGING TREE

TOWARDS MONKS MOUND ←

● THE GOLDEN FARM

LONELY CLOWN'S SHACK ●

● RAT KID'S LAIR
● TROLL'S CAVE

SPELL CHAMBER ●

SWAN LADY'S HOME ●

ENTRANCE TO
THE OTHERLANDS

THE EMBANKMENT

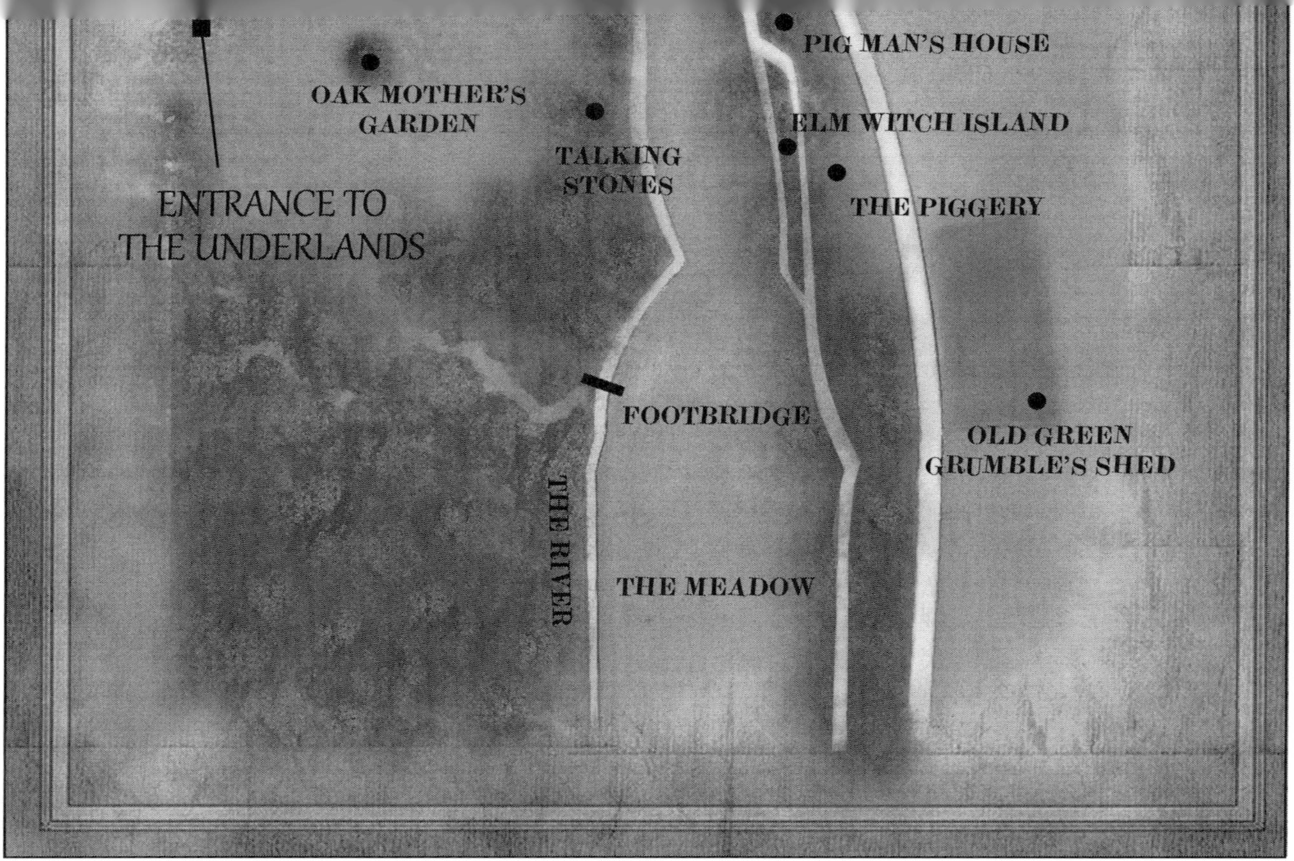

ENTRANCE TO
THE UNDERLANDS
OAK MOTHER'S
GARDEN
TALKING
STONES
PIG MAN'S HOUSE
ELM WITCH ISLAND
THE PIGGERY
FOOTBRIDGE
OLD GREEN
GRUMBLE'S SHED
THE RIVER
THE MEADOW

CHAPTER 1

THE SUMMER FLOOD

It was early evening. The sun was about to disappear behind the trees standing watch from the old railway embankment.

"We ought to go back now, it'll be dark soon." I was struggling to unknot the laces of my soaking wet shoes.

"Just five more minutes," said Hewett and he disappeared beneath the water.

Normally the stream barely covered our knees, but following two days of thunder storms the water was threatening to spill over into the surrounding meadow. The stream was now wide enough that we could take a decent run-up to the edge of the bank and turn a full somersault, before landing in the water. It was clear enough that we could see stones and patches of weed on the bottom and any crayfish that might have come scuttling towards our feet.

My eye followed the stream as it flowed toward the culvert and into the darkness of the tunnel. I shuddered at the thought of what was lurking there in the shadows, picking spiders off the walls and crunching them between long yellow teeth.

I could just make out the opening at the other side of the embankment, where the stream carried on its journey under the gas pipe and into the copse.

"Come on, I'm freezing now, let's go," I said, as Hewett re-surfaced.

"It's not cold, you wimp!"

"My mum will go mental if I miss tea again."

"Oh, alright then, I'm starving anyway." He climbed out of the stream and on to the bank, where we spent some time pulling on our wet shoes with the laces still tied.

We set off for home, giggling at the squelching sounds made by our shoes. We followed the river to where it disappeared into a conduit, passing beneath the road and reappearing in the wooded glade where it split in two, forming a thin island. That was where the Elm Witch lived.

In the half-light of the setting sun, I looked to see if she was there, scratching about in the foliage, gathering figwort and hart's-tongue and other ingredients for her foul-smelling potions. There was no sign today.

We carried on, past the big grey house and the pig sheds, and up to the footbridge over the dual carriageway. We could see the rough square of allotment gardens and the rising trail of smoke that carried the stench of cabbage leaves. The Old Green Grumble would be there, hidden away in his shed, waiting to pounce on any trespassing children.

The footbridge ended at a steep grassy slope, and without hesitation, we rolled down it, climbed back up, then rolled down a second time. We gathered ourselves and began advancing across the stretch of wasteland that lay ahead. In no time at all, we were in full battle mode, charging at the invisible enemy rising to meet us.

We came to the houses at the edge of the Kingshill estate and stopped under the rowan tree to catch our breath. Walking to school last autumn I'd met a group of people standing in this same spot, looking up into the branches, focusing their binoculars on the group of birds roosting there. The birds were a soft grey colour with a touch of dusky pink.

"What are they?" I asked.

"Waxwings," replied the twitcher nearest to me. "Don't normally see them this far west."

It sounded to me as if the birds were squabbling among themselves, casting blame on whichever one had led them in the wrong direction. It reminded me of holidays in Wales, with Mum trying to read the map and Dad driving around endless narrow lanes, wondering whether we'd ever reach the bed and breakfast before dark.

"Come on then, I'll race you," said Hewett and he set off at pace, heading up Queen Elizabeth Road.

I chased after him and by the time we'd reached the top of the hill, it was neck and neck. As we approached the finish line Hewett found one last surge of energy and inched ahead of me. He reached the post box outside my house and slammed his hands against it.

"The winner is Hewett," he shouted, raising both arms victoriously and jumping up and down as if basking in the applause of an ecstatic crowd. With my lungs burning and my stomach groaning, I bid farewell.

"See you tomorrow then?" I panted.

"Yeah probably, although my mum wants me to get some new trainers, so I'll have to wait until I get back from town," sighed Hewett, clearly not relishing the prospect.

"OK then, just call round when you're ready," I said, as I ran down the steps to my front door.

"Yeah, okay, see ya!" said Hewett.

"See ya!"

After dinner, having wolfed down the plate that my mother had reheated for me and said goodnight to her and Dad, I dragged my aching limbs upstairs. The bathroom mirror showed that my face was now salmon pink where the sun had gently baked my skin. I half-stumbled into my bedroom, where my brother, Nick, was lying on his bed, headphones on, listening to his Walkman. I could hear him singing along quietly, and I recognised the words to *Mr Clean* by the Jam. He was making a bleeping sound in place of the swear words.

"Night," I said, regardless of whether he could hear me, and I lay down on my bed with a blissful sigh. I closed my eyes and felt as though my entire body was still bathed in sunlight. The smell of the stream still clung to my skin and hair. I recalled the names of the plants growing along the banks – bladder-sedge, mare's tail, dwarf spikerush, bog stitchwort; more ingredients for the Elm Witch's potions I thought, before the golden haze behind my eyes changed to a muddy green and I smiled with relief. Sleep would come easily to me tonight.

CHAPTER 2

CARTOON TIME

I woke in a panic, thinking I'd overslept and was late for school – then I remembered it was Saturday. I tore around my room, assembling a cleanish set of clothes to wear for the day; blue Terry Towelling shorts, Starsky & Hutch t-shirt, white socks and the brown lace up daps that were still wet from yesterday. Hewett would still be in bed, and soon he'd be dragged off to buy trainers with his mum. Then he'd be hungry so he'd have to go for a Wimpy lunch which meant he wouldn't be home until at least one o'clock, and I wasn't going to wait that long.

I ran downstairs into the kitchen where my mother stood at the sink, wringing out a pair of football shorts.

"Morning, lovely boy. Did you sleep ok? No horrible dreams?"

I shook my head while I filled a bowl with my favourite cereal: Golden Nuggets. I kept one eye on the television in the front room – heroes, Gods and villains, animals and scarecrows appearing in dreamlike visions on the screen, shrieking and laughing while committing acts of extreme violence towards each other.

"Your dad and I have been worried about you," said Mum, as she mopped up the puddle of milk I'd left on the counter.

Dad was manager of Chesterton under 12s, so Saturday mornings always involved carting nine or so kids about in his Austin Allegro, the boot stuffed with sets of football shirts, socks and shorts. Mum always packed a couple of Tupperware tubs filled with orange quarters for half time. Sometimes I would tag along. I wasn't particularly interested in watching the game, although there was always the prospect of a fight breaking out between the players, or a disgruntled parent swearing at the referee for making a bad decision.

"Have you tidied your room?" asked Mum, working at the mud-caked bundle in the sink. "*This* is your brother's football kit. He's just told me he needs it for today's match. It's been in a carrier bag under his bed all week."

Queen's *Fat Bottomed Girls* started to play on the Bakelite radio next to her. She immediately turned up the volume.

"Lunch will be ready at one o'clock," she called as I opened the front door to leave, in a way that suggested there would be no debate on the matter.

"OK, see you at one then."

"See you lovely boy," she replied, before bursting into song again. "Get on your bikes and ride!" she shouted, punching the air in true Freddie style. I shook my head and left her to it.

I made my way out into the back garden and stepped through the gap in the fence. Here I could look down on the stretch of disused railway line that once ran between City Bank and where Kingshill school now stood. Where once the tracks had been there was now a wide footpath, flanked on either side by steep banks, covered in goosegrass, dog rose and hawthorn. On the side nearest my house, a path had been worn through the undergrowth and the hawthorn branches arched overhead to create a tunnel. I started walking and the morning sunlight came spattering through the leaves and branches, creating a spectacular mirrorball effect.

I started to run, as if I was being chased by an unseen terror; an elemental force born of the Underworld, hunting down another hapless soul to be dragged beneath the soil, condemned to live out my days in the damp and dark realms where worms and chucky pigs[1] carry out their work.

By the time I'd reached the end of the path, my heart was hammering and my mind was racing but I kept going. I passed the Golden Farm pub and stopped myself from glancing at the upstairs window, where the ghost of the Golden Farmer had been known to appear. I remembered the story my grandad had told me, how hundreds of years ago, the Golden Farmer had lived a

---

[1] Chucky pigs: local name given to woodlice. Variations include pill bugs, cheese logs and roly-polys.

double life; farmer by day and highwayman by night.

"Turns out he got caught in the end and was hanged from that tree at the end of your road," said Grandad, referring to the old oak tree that stands on the green not fifty yards from my house.[2]

From then on, if ever I found myself walking past the tree, I was sure to keep my eyes to the ground for fear of seeing the farmer's lifeless body gently swinging in the branches above.

At last, I turned on to the grass track leading down to the meadow and felt a familiar shimmer of joy as I took in the sight of City Bank basking in the lemon sherbet glow of the summer morning. There was the

---

[2] An account in the *Wilts and Gloucestershire Standard* from 1953, when the pub opened, states that William Davis (originally from Wales) lived there with his wife and 18 children. He was prosperous, despite the large family, and the fact that the farm was a poor one puzzled the local inhabitants. About the same time a local gang of Highwaymen, who had headquarters in the Hamlet of Ready Token (7 miles east of Cirencester), flourished in the neighbourhood and their nefarious activities obliged the forces of law and order to make a midnight swoop on the district. The gang was rounded up and when the leader was unmasked, he proved to be none other than the Golden Farmer. Over many years he had robbed coaches, mostly near Salisbury but also in London, where he was eventually apprehended and committed to Newgate. Records from the Newgate trials calendar state that on Friday 20 December 1689, at the age of 64, Davis was executed at Salisbury Court in Fleet Street. Afterwards his body was hanged in chains on Bagshot Heath.

stream giggling its way along one side of the meadow, with a few children swimming in the sparkling water. Others were using nets to catch snottygogs[3], before tipping them into jam jars to take a close look at them. The children pulled faces, mimicking the gulping mouths of the tiny fish.

I noticed that a group of older kids were heading up to the top of the railway embankment where they would smoke cigarettes out of sight of prying eyes. The wood trolls that lived on the other side of the embankment would be sleeping in their troll hole right now, digesting last night's feast. I shuddered, imagining their gurning faces as they chomped on whatever they had managed to scavenge in the darkness; the swallowing sounds they made as the food slid down into those swollen troll bellies. I jumped out of my skin when I heard the screams of a child.

It was nothing. She had fallen off the end of the slide and her mother was already spitting onto a tissue, ready to apply time honoured treatment to knee and elbow. The playground, built on a wide strip of concrete, presented a range of potential hazards, whether it was a foot caught under the spinning roundabout or friction burns from the blazing hot surface of the slide. Parents were on constant alert, listening out for the cries of their child like adult penguins, singling out the call of

---

[3] Snottygogs or snottydogs: local name given to European bullheads, small freshwater fish, with large head and fins and tapering body. Also known as *millers' thumbs*.

their young from the crowd.

I received a thump to the back of my head. I looked behind me and there was Darren, laughing and clutching the football he'd just thrown at me.

"Alright Skins? Not with Gobby today then?"

"Takes one to know one," I replied.

"Ooh, you're *funny*," said Darren. "Anyway, good job he's not here, else I'd kick his head in!"

"Why, what's he done to you?" I asked.

"He's so flippin' full of himself, thinks he's better than the rest of us."

"No he doesn't. Just leave him alone." My voice was wobbling a bit, and I didn't sound nearly as tough as I wanted to.

"Or what?" Darren grinned. "You gonna beat me up?"

"Nah, can't be bothered." I said, realising I was pushing my luck. I braced myself for a quick getaway.

"Oi, Darren, I've got a bone to pick with you!" came the voice of Darren's neighbour, Mr Sharpe. "How many times do I have to ask you not to kick that damn ball against the side of my house?"

"It wasn't me," said Darren.

"You must think I'm as stupid as you are. Just don't do it again, or I'll have to have a word with your dad."

"Go ahead, my dad could beat you up any day," replied Darren.

This seemed like the ideal opportunity to make my escape.

I climbed the steps onto the top of the embankment. The path where the train track had once run was a narrow line between thorn bushes and brambles, their pale pink flowers floating like fairies sent to tame the fury.

I hesitated, cautious; checking there were no older kids up ahead, smoking and looking to pick fights with other kids. The rivalry between the two secondary schools was fierce. Confrontations were common up here, ending in many a black eye, nosebleed or fat lip. I was even more terrified of falling foul of the group of Punks who'd claimed the area as their territory. I'd heard stories of Punks chucking little kids into the large bed of stinging nettles found at the far end of the embankment – the snake-pit.

But this was where I meant to come today. This was the place that called to me, time and time again.

I stepped through a gap in the undergrowth. I clambered down the steep slope of the embankment and came to the place where the river appeared from the tunnel. It carried on its course through the copse, between the soft greens of hazel and willow. The ground was peppered with pieces of junk that had somehow found their way there; paint buckets, chicken wire, the odd fridge and rusting sheets of corrugated metal, some of which had been used to make the shack where the Lonely Clown lived.

The gas pipeline crossed the stream here and I couldn't resist walking across it, just to prove I could without falling off. I remembered the time Justin slipped and crashed down onto the pipe, smashing the side of his head, which caused a sickening chiming noise, like Big Ben sounding one o'clock. Justin was lying face down in the stream and three of us rushed in to drag him out. We helped him up onto the bank, where he sat slumped like an old teddy bear. He opened his eyes and clutched the sides of his head, groaning softly.

"You alright mate?" I said.

"Yeah, I think I'm alright," he replied.

"You had us worried for a second."

"Bit of a headache," he added, before suddenly remembering something and putting his hand in his trouser pocket.

"Oh flippin'eck!" he said, holding up a dripping wad of Star Wars bubble gum cards. He tried to separate them, but they'd become soggy, and disintegrated like a Rich Tea biscuit in a hot cup of tea.

Today, I was alone and listening to the sounds that surrounded me; birdsong, the babbling stream, the distant shouts of children playing on the other side of the embankment and the ever-present hiss of traffic drifting over from the dual carriageway. I climbed the monkey arm tree and crawled along the branch that stretched out over the stream. I sat staring down at the water.

"I'm not afraid of you," I called out into the surroundings. "You'll see. I'm going to stay here until my friends arrive. I'm not going to run away." My voice was shaking.

I could only have been there for a minute or two when I became aware of a presence nearby. I looked out of the corner of my eye and there at the mouth of the culvert, stood a girl, dressed in simple clothes, her face framed by peach coloured hair.

The shock shot through me and I braced. My chest was heaving as I drew in short sharp breaths.

"Who are you," I shouted, "Tell me your name."

Just then, the sound of voices came from the other direction. I watched as the girl turned and ran, disappearing into the trees and undergrowth on the other side of the stream.

"Who are you talking to?" It was Hewett. He and Michael came bounding along the pathway towards me.

"No one, just myself."

"You're such a looney," said Michael.

"Takes one to know one. Anyway, what kept you both?" I said, diverting attention away from myself.

"New trainers," said Hewett, looking down at his spanking new pair of Adidas Kick.

"Lush." I said, slightly jealous because I knew my daps were made by a cheap brand no one had heard of.

"Right then, what shall we do?" said Michael.

"My brother reckons there's a new Tarzan swing the other end of the railway bank," Hewett said as casually as he could.

"Tarzan swing. How old are you, five?" I laughed.

"I didn't say I wanted to go on it," replied Hewett.

"Bagsy I get first go!" said Michael, affecting a squeaky baby voice and he started off up the bank. I raced after him, leaving Hewett behind. He was struggling to get a good foothold; the slope had become slippery with all the recent rain.

"Hurry up Hewett, it'll be dark before you get to the top," said Michael. We waited as Hewett clambered up the bank and stepped out from the shadow of the undergrowth. He stood staring down at his trainers, which were now covered in thick dark mud.

"My mum's going to kill me," he sighed.

There was no sign of anyone as the three of us sprinted along the track, the white flowers of cow parsley exploding like tiny silent fireworks on either side. Red Admiral butterflies sunned their wings while fuzzy bees buzzed drowsily. If the girl had come this way, she'd left no sign.

"Who are you looking for?" demanded Hewett.

"No one."

Michael was pointing to the blue nylon rope hanging from a tree growing a little way down from the top of embankment. He was the fastest runner and got to the rope first. A thick piece of wood had been fastened to the end, acting as a handlebar or a seat, and a series of knots provided grips for grubby hands to clasp. The other end of the rope was lashed to a branch high above us, and I marvelled at the fact that someone had managed to climb to that point.

Michael leaned out to grab the rope, and once he had hold of it, adjusting his grip around two of the knots, he stepped back and with his arms fully stretched he threw himself forward. In a single movement he picked up his legs and straddled the wooden bar as he swung out over the embankment, the ground now ten feet below him, before arcing back towards us, a look of sheer delight upon his face. As Michael's feet regained the top of the slope, Hewett and I reached for the rope, and held it steady as he climbed off the seat.

"My turn," said Hewett, taking a couple of steps backwards before launching himself over the brow. He tried to straddle the bar mid-flight, but couldn't manage it, and as the swing reached the apex of its arc, Hewett lost his grip.

For a brief moment, his arms were paddling the air, frantically trying to right himself. But his legs had swung out in front of him, his body was almost perpendicular to the ground. He landed on his side, his ribs and shoulder taking the full impact. He lay there, at the foot of the slope, half submerged in a bed of ivy, gasping for breath, the wind knocked clean out of him.

Michael and I scrambled down the bank to where Hewett was lying foetal-like, moaning softly.

"Wow, that was amazing," I said. "You were like Spider Man for a second."

"Shut up, it's not funny," said Hewett.

"Just the landing that needs a bit of work," said

Michael, and the two of us started sniggering. I could see Hewett was trying not to smile, but in the end he gave up and started laughing, which caused him to wince.

"Don't make me laugh, it hurts." He sat up, leaves and twigs poking out of his hair, his hands reddened from rope burns. We helped him to his feet, a vision of dishevelment.

"Shall we have another go?" asked Michael hopefully.

"No, I'd better go back for my lunch," I said.

"Me too, I'm starving," said Hewett, and we headed back towards the stream, so that he could wash the mud off his trainers. He dipped a handful of dock leaves in the water and used them to wipe the dirt from his shoes. Satisfied with the result, he slipped them back on and we set off for the flyover.

"I wonder if the Swan Lady is there?" said Michael, looking down the slope towards the river, where half-submerged shopping trollies and traffic cones lay floundered. Beyond, lay the copse where the Swan Lady worked, tending to her injured birds and critters. The swans were easy to spot through the foliage, wafting about in their pens as a few ducks pattered amongst them. On a good day, I'd be stopped in my tracks by the sound of the peacock.

"She's probably brewing up some poison, to put into toffee apples, ready for Halloween," I said.

"I heard she caught a kid sneaking in, about to steal one of the peacock's feathers," said Hewett. "She tried to drown him in the pond."

"Which kid?" asked Michael.

"My brother's friend's brother, I think. Anyway, another kid nearly had his eyes pecked out by one of her crows."

"Really?" said Michael.

"Yes, really," said Hewett picking up pace with Michael and I following close behind. We tore across the flyover passing the point where usually we would have stopped to flob spit over the rails on to the dual carriageway below. This time we kept moving, keen to leave the copse behind us.

We carried on past the Golden Farm pub, its upper windows dark and empty and only once the houses of Queen Elizabeth Road had come into view, did we feel it was safe to stop running. We stood for a minute or so, chests heaving and brows glistening with sweat. Charged with adrenaline, the three of us started laughing before turning our heads up to the sky and howling like wolves. Walking back together along the railway line towards the bridge, my mind began drifting.

"Do you believe in other worlds?" I asked, quite out of the blue.

"What are you on about?" said Hewett,

"You know, worlds beyond this one." I was trying to be matter of fact.

"What, like other planets?"

"No, I mean other dimensions."

"Like The Twilight Zone?" said Hewett, and in

unison, he and Michael broke out into an uncanny rendition of the theme music. *"Ning-ning-ning-ning ning-ning-ning-ning."*

"I'm being serious. What if there really are other worlds, and some of us can actually go there?"

"You've been watching too much telly."

"OK, where do ghosts come from then?"

"Ghosts aren't real."

"My Gran swears she saw a ghost when she was little. She said one night, there was an old woman sat on the end of her bed, and it wasn't her mum or anything," said Michael.

"Don't tell me. You've seen a ghost," said Hewett.

"No, I haven't," I said, trying to convince myself as much as anyone.

"So what's this all about then?"

"Nothing, just ignore me. Anyway, I have to go home now, see you tomorrow."

"See ya!" they replied, and as I walked away they started singing, *"ning-ning-ning-ning-ning-ning-ning."* I flicked the Vs over my shoulder and carried on walking.

CHAPTER 3

A BAD DREAM

Arriving home, as I approached our front door, I found the family cats, Charcoal and Sid, were stuck in the cat flap. I could see their heads and upper halves wedged together, front legs straining to reach the ground, their jet black fur covered with patches of white powder.

After a few moments of intense struggle, with much hissing and grumbling, I managed to pull Charcoal through, with Sid spilling out after him. They each scuttled off, keeping low to the ground, all wild eyes and ruffled fur.

I opened the kitchen door and there, in a cloud of flea powder, stood my dad, nursing deep red scratches that ran half the length of his arm. The lenses of his glasses were completely white and after wiping them clean with his handkerchief, he spat into the sink, clearing his mouth and throat. Finally he took out his handkerchief and blew his nose noisily.

"You've de-flead the cats then?" I was trying hard

not to laugh.

"Well, I think your father got more of it than they did. The lid came off, and it went everywhere," said mum, stifling her giggles. "Then the cats tried to escape through the cat flap at the same time." At this point she lost control and tears of laughter rolled down her cheeks.

"Very funny." mumbled Dad, as he opened one kitchen cupboard after another, searching for the first aid box.

That evening, after tea, I made myself a SodaStream cherryade and took it with me as I headed outside. Our house was set to one side of a bridge where the road passed over the old railway line. I climbed over our garden wall and dropped down on to the concrete ledge that jutted out of the bridge's underside, a good three meters above the old track bed.

Here was a good place for spotting butterflies and I'd become obsessed with one type in particular; the swallowtail. I pictured its yellow and black marbled wings with those red and blue markings like eyes, staring back at any potential predator and the black tails that stream behind its lower wings. Even though there was little chance of it happening in this part of the country, I would often venture out, armed with my net and plastic camera, hoping to spot one. Of course, Darren claimed to have seen one in his backyard, but we all knew he was lying. The sighting of a swallowtail had become, for me, some sort of Holy Grail, the equivalent of finding Mario Kempes in a packet of Panini World Cup stickers.

Where do all the butterflies go when it gets dark, I thought to myself. Do they sleep and if so how come moths come out at night? I shuffled along to the end of the ledge and sat with my back to the wall. I dangled my legs over the edge, the ground a long way below me and took several long swigs of my drink. The sweet flavour exploded in a thousand tiny bubbles, like cartoon violence on my tongue. I drank some more and after a satisfyingly loud belch, I started thinking about the girl with peach coloured hair, and the way she'd disappeared just before Hewett and Michael arrived. She wasn't like the other strangers. She'd looked like any other kid. Perhaps she had fangs or a forked tongue. Maybe she lived in the snake-pit.

It was then that I noticed how dark it had become. The light from the streetlamps lent the sky a butterscotch glow. I began hurriedly shuffling back along the ledge towards the bank. I don't know why I am such a wimp, scared all the time, crying when I think no one can see.

I looked up and there in the mouth of the tree tunnel, was the girl. I gasped loudly.

"I'm so sorry, I didn't mean to startle you," she said.

"Who are you?" I clambered up to stand with my back against the side of the bridge.

"My name is Aislinn," she said, and gently bowed her head.

"I'm Steven, and that's my house right there." I

pointed towards the house, on the other side of the fence. The kitchen light was off so I knew my parents must be in the front room, watching television. No use calling out to them.

"It was you I saw down by the gas pipe wasn't it?" I said.

"Yes it was." As she spoke, I noticed there were no fangs or forked tongue. I could see her face was peppered with freckles and her pale green eyes looked out from beneath a slightly uneven fringe. Her dark red shoes were heavily scuffed and the buckles were rusted.

"Why did you run off when my friends turned up?" I asked.

"I didn't know who they were," she replied.

I was about to ask her which school she went to when Mum called from the kitchen. "In you come now. Bedtime soon."

Aislinn disappeared as quickly as she had before. This time, at least she waved goodbye as she hurried back into the hawthorn tunnel.

"Meet me here, tomorrow morning," I shouted after her, but I wasn't sure she could hear me.

I climbed over the wall and went back inside the house, through the kitchen and into the living room. Mum, Dad and Nick were watching the news, in which Kit Williams was talking about his book *Masquerade*. The book was full of illustrations and verse containing clues about the whereabouts of the Golden Hare jewel, which had been buried in the ground somewhere in

England. My head reeled with thoughts of tangled roots and creatures crawling and slithering among them.

"Who was that you were talking to? I've not seen her before," said Mum.

"Ooooooohhhh, was it your girlfriend?" said Nick, sticking his finger into his mouth as if to make himself throw up.

"Shut up will you," I shouted before storming upstairs to my room. I slumped down on my bed and lay there, arms folded staring up at the ceiling light. There was a tap on the door.

"Are you alright lovey?" came Mum's voice.

"Yeah, I'm alright thanks Mum. I'm just tired, that's all."

Mum poked her head round the door. "Your brother was only pulling your leg. Don't take everything so seriously." she said, kissing me on the top of my head. She left, closing the door behind her. I was too tired to change into my pyjamas so I lay on the bed, still fully clothed. I put my head against the pillow and after a while my eyelids began to close.

I was hurrying down the disused road, milk-white blossom and cow parsley blurring as I sped past. I came to the bottom of the track, where the railway arch rose out of the undergrowth. In the twilight I could just make out the figure looking down at me, murmuring as I passed below. My feet seemed to be floating just above the ground and I moved effortlessly across the footbridge and over the battlefield until I arrived at the building site. As I passed the half-built houses, I saw blurred faces staring out at me through the empty windows. In no time at all I found myself standing at the end of the playing field, looking over the wheat growing tall and straight. The sheaths wavered slightly as figures moved through them, heading in the direction of Monk's Mound.

The moon's soft silvery sheen suddenly changed to a harsh white glare and I was back in my room. My brother rummaging around under his bed.

"Turn the light off," I said, "I was almost asleep then."

"Sorry, just need to find my swimming trunks," he said. "We're going to the outdoor pool tomorrow, are you coming?"

"Nah, I've got some stuff I need to do here," I said.

"Really? Everyone will be there."

"No you're alright. I think I've got a bit of a cold coming anyway."

"A cold? It's August!" He rummaged a bit more, bringing clothes, comics and all sorts of paraphernalia out from under the bed until finally, he found his pair of trunks. He shoved all the other items back under his bed and left the room, shouting as he went, "Mum, where are the towels?"

I got out of bed, huffing in frustration and turned off the light. I climbed back into bed and lay there, wide awake, my mind a busy place, bustling with shadows and whispers.

CHAPTER 4

THE DAWN CHORUS

Morning had barely broken. The birds and I had the world to ourselves and the air around me was filled with their songs. I was back at the spot where Aislinn had left me yesterday evening, standing at the mouth of the hawthorn tunnel.

"Hello," I said, loud enough to be heard but not so loud as to draw too much attention to myself. "Hello, are you there?"

There suddenly came a rustling sound nearby. I looked to see a hundred or so newspaper pages floating down from the top of the bridge. It was quite common for paperboys and girls to dump their surplus copies over the bridge rather than lug them back to the newsagents. Some pages had become snagged in the thistles and were flapping in the gentle breeze. I followed one as it wafted and whorled along the length of the track, as far as the small electricity substation at the end, where it became caught on one of the fence's tall metal spikes.

Then I heard a sound of cracking twigs coming from inside the hawthorn tunnel, and there, walking towards me, was Aislinn. For a few moments, we stood staring at the ground, not knowing what to say to each other. It was Aislinn who spoke first.

"You've seen them, haven't you?" she said and my heart started thumping in my chest.

"I don't know what you mean," I said, shifting uncomfortably on the spot.

"I heard you calling out to them, when you were up in the tree," said Aislinn.

"I was calling to my friends," I replied but Aislinn simply raised her eyebrows to suggest she was not convinced. She folded her arms and fixed me with a rather fierce expression. I sighed, knowing she wasn't going to fall for my lies. "You must think I'm a looney."

"No, not at all. In fact, you and I are very similar," replied Aislinn. It took me a few seconds to work out what she meant by this.

Finally, I said, "You've seen them too?"

"Yes I have," said Aislinn and she sat down on the trunk of a fallen tree. I sat next to her and she began talking to me about the shadowy figures that would appear to her, not only in her dreams but in broad daylight too. She told me they are called the Unseen. I was dumbstruck. Here was a girl that I had only just met, sharing the same strange experiences as me. I felt a sense of relief, knowing I wasn't alone. I then heard myself talking as if a muzzle had finally been removed from my mouth. I told her how they would always appear whenever I was alone, walking home from school or playing under the railway bridge. Sometimes I would look out of my bedroom window and there would be one of them, standing at the end of the garden, staring up at me. I told Aislinn about the drawings I had made of them and how terrifying it was to see the figures emerge from the page. I told her it felt as though I'd been possessed.

"There is someone I know who can help us" said Aislinn. "She's friendly. She can make them go away, the nightmares I mean."

"Who is she, does she live round here?" I asked.

"Sort of," replied Aislinn.

"What do you mean, sort of?" Aislinn paused before answering.

"She lives in a place called the Otherlands."

"The Otherlands? Is that where they've built all those new houses?" I asked.

"No," said Aislinn, "It's a whole other world. It's separated from our world by a thin veil and there is a tear in that veil. That's how I got into the Otherlands, through the tear. I was out playing along the embankment one day and I just stumbled across it."

"I think my head's going to explode," I said.

"Sorry," said Aislinn "I've been keeping this a secret for a while, it's all pouring out of me now." She took a deep breath before continuing.

"I can take you to the Otherlands and introduce you to the Oak Mother. She was the one that found me when I first went there. I can't wait for you to meet her, she has all these incredible books full of remedies and spells."

"Hang on, spells? You mean, magic spells?" I gasped.

"Yes, magic spells," said Aislinn excitedly. My head was spinning.

"I need some time to think about it," I said.

"Of course. I understand. It's a lot to take in." She stood up slowly and walked over to the hawthorn tunnel. She turned back towards me.

"We could meet at the steps by the railway arch at City Bank. Monday morning, if you like?" Aislinn sounded almost apologetic, as if she'd just opened a whole can of worms and poured them over my head.

"Okay," I replied, still dazed. Aislinn waved goodbye and walked away through the hawthorn tunnel. I stood for a minute or so trying to regain my composure. I watched as an old man passed by walking his dog along the railway line. A kid came from the other direction wheeling his bike, the front tyre flat. Probably some broken glass under the bridge. The sound of birdsong had been replaced by the distant roar of cars weaving their way from A to B. The church bells rang out in the distance. It should have felt like any other Sunday morning, but for me it felt like nothing would ever be normal again.

CHAPTER 5

RUNNERS AND SEEKERS

Later that afternoon, a group of us congregated at the Green Thing, a rectangular structure that stood on the patch of grass between Golden Farm Road and Crabtree Lane. The Green Thing was slightly taller than Martin, who was by far the tallest of our group, and it was wide enough that children could chase each other around it.

No one seemed to know what this pea green, metal monolith was or what purpose it served. Maybe it was something to do with the electricity substation that stood not ten metres away but that didn't stop us from climbing up and sitting on top of it. Indeed the twins, Leah and Sarah were already doing just that and from their commanding position they had started organising the rest of us into two teams.[4]

Martin and my brother Nick had been designated

---

[4] The green thing was the property of Regent Oil Company. It housed the pumps that fed oil from the tanks below to the surrounding houses for heating. Eventually it turned out to be too costly so it was shut down. It still stands there today.

team leaders and after much shouting and pushing the rest of us joined our respective sides. After further squabbling and deliberation it was decided that Martin would lead the runners and Nick would lead the seekers. Michael, Hewett and I took our places alongside Martin. The twins jumped down from the Green Thing and joined their fellow seekers.

Runners and seekers was a glorified version of hide and seek, in which one group went off to hide and the other group came to find them. Once a member of the 'runners' had been found they had to join the rest of the seekers in their hunt. The last runner to be found was the winner. The sheer expanse of the housing estates meant that seekers could be searching indefinitely, and games were more often than not abandoned after a couple of hours.

"Runners get ready," yelled Nick, prompting a tumultuous countdown from the rest of his team.

10 … 9 … 8 … 7 … 6 … 5 … 4 … 3 … 2 … 1

To the sound of excited cheers and jeers, the other runners and I set off at a frantic pace, scattering in every direction, trying to lose ourselves within the labyrinth of houses and pathways. The sound of the seekers counting from one to a hundred faded as Hewett and I skirted close to the edge of the building site.

"Mum'll kill me if we hide in there," said Hewett, tugging the sleeve of my t-shirt.

"Mine too," I said.

But I knew the seekers would already be on their

way and I didn't want to be the first to be caught. In a moment of madness, I left the path and headed across the compacted mud to one of the half-built houses.

"I'm going to get in to so much trouble," said Hewett as he reluctantly joined me.

I gingerly stepped in through the opening that would at some point become the front door. We hadn't been seen.

I walked across the solid cement floor to the skeletal wooden staircase in the far corner. Hewett followed me as I climbed the stairs, leaving an incriminating trail of muddy footprints behind us.

At the top of the stairs was the landing, a stretch of bare wooden floorboards off of which led three empty doorways. I peered into the nearest doorway and looked down through the bare rafters to the concrete floor below. Ignoring my mum's warnings echoing inside my head, I took the first few steps along one of the rafters.

"What are you doing?" shouted Hewett, "You'll break your neck if you fall."

"They'll never find us here," I said, and remembering the trick used by tight rope walkers, I looked straight ahead at the point I was aiming towards. With great relief, I made it to the empty window space set in the outside wall. Balancing on the rafter, I crouched down and looked out of the window. From my vantage point, I could see anyone arriving from the right, at the Crabtree Lane end and from North Home Road to my left.

After some hesitation, Hewett crossed the rafters and joined me at the window.

"This is brilliant," he said. "We can see them coming a mile off."

After a few minutes my knees started to ache and I carefully sat with my legs hanging down into the room below.

Just then something moved beneath me. I looked down through the rafters and saw a figure walking through the doorway and over to the staircase. The figure looked to be wearing a long black tailcoat and a hat adorned on each side with black and white feathers. Without thinking I clambered through the window space and clinging to the sill I lowered my body down the wall until my feet were dangling two meters from the ground.

"What's wrong?" came Hewett's voice from inside the building but I was in too much of a panic to reply. I dropped to the ground, the soft mud cushioning my fall. I got to my feet and hurried across the site, leaping over the trenches, dodging the piles of bricks and scaffolding poles.

The mud had caked to the bottom of my shoes, making running far more difficult but the fear was surging through me, driving me on. As I reached the bottom of the road leading up to my house I slowed down. Checking over my shoulder, I stood at the top of the steps at the front of my house. I waited a minute or so for my breathing to return to normal. I dragged my feet back and forth along the tarmac, scraping off the mud from my shoes, and walked down the steps to my front door, preparing my excuses for why I'd come home by myself.

I could hear the sound of the lawn mower coming from the back garden and mum shouting to be heard over it. This meant the house was empty and hopefully I would avoid any awkward questions. I rushed in and headed straight up to my room. I sat at my desk and without thinking I opened my sketch pad. Using a black colouring pencil my hand moving rapidly over the paper, I began creating a series of jagged lines. Soon the page was covered with a seething mass of black thorns, in the centre of which sat a small hunched figure, its arms clasped around its knees, head buried, helpless to the chaos that was closing in around it.

CHAPTER 6

GRAN AND GRANDAD

Dad, Mum, Nick and I were travelling to Cheltenham on our regular Sunday visit to Gran and Grandad. It was a relief to leave the morning behind me and arguing about whether we should play I-Spy or the car colour game[5] came as a welcome distraction.

We pulled up outside the familiar terraced house, and there was Gran, on her hands and knees, cloth in hand, polishing the doorstep. It was a habit she'd never managed to break, since the time when neighbours used to routinely comment on the slightest shortfall in the upkeep of one's home. Gran would also iron her dusters – instilled into her from her years of service as a scullery maid, which began at the tender age of fourteen. She would often tell me about these years, how she was servant to the servants, the 'lowest of the low.'

---

[5] The car colour game involved each passenger choosing a colour and keeping score of how many cars of that colour passed in the opposite direction (red and blue being the most popular choices). Cheating was rife as each player could be very liberal in keeping their own score.

"At five o'clock every morning," she'd say, "the head butler would put on a pair of white gloves and run his fingers over the top of the mantlepiece. Any dirt would show up on his gloves, you see, and Heaven help us if we'd missed a bit."

Then there was the time when she'd been washing the linen using carbolic soap. "It pretty much stripped the skin from my hands and arms. One of the older maids took me into town, to the chemists. He gave me this ointment to put on, and oh my word how it burned. I wept and wept all through the night, then they docked my pay for the time I was out. Still, the sores cleared up soon after that."

Gran shook the cloth she'd been using to clean the stone doorstep, and folded it neatly back into the pocket of her apron.

"You don't have to do that any more, remember?" said my mum as she helped Gran up.

'Doesn't do any harm," Gran said wincing as her knees clicked loudly.

My brother and I walked in through the front door and were immediately met by the comforting smells of furniture polish, paraffin from the brass lamps and baking from the kitchen. Gran always managed to keep us occupied, whether it was polishing the silverware, picking out weeds from the garden path or taking the empty pop bottles back to the shop to collect a refund. Today though, we were ushered straight into the front room.

"Now then, here comes trouble." Grandad gave his standard greeting as he sat in his armchair, the little table in front of him upon which he had arranged his assorted essential items. There was the chunky TV remote control, the back of which was held on with Sellotape, his copy of the Daily Mirror open at the horseracing pages and a small plastic Ladbrokes pen next to it.

He kept his lazy tongs close by, so that he could pick up anything that might have dropped on to the floor without having to leave his seat.[6] There was also a golden syrup tin filled with rubber bands. Grandad might stop mid conversation, pick a rubber band from the tin, wrap one end over his thumb and forefinger, take aim and release, sending the rubber band shooting across the room or up at the ceiling to where an unsuspecting housefly would be taking a short rest.

"Bingo!" he'd cry as yet another victim dropped to the floor.

As always, mealtime was quite the event. There was a huge roast dinner followed by pudding, later followed by a teatime spread and more pudding and yet another pot of tea, covered with one of Gran's hand knitted tea cosies. As the others chatted in the kitchen, I moved

---

[6] Lazy tongs: used for grasping objects at a distance. (Grandad would often use them to reach across the table to pick up a rock bun or sandwich during mealtimes, much to Gran's disapproval. Also known as 'ember tongs', used for picking up hot embers from a fireplace.

over to where Grandad was sitting in his armchair.

"How are you doing, kid?" he asked. "Your mum said that you've still been getting nightmares?"

I gave a small nod. Grandad made a sympathetic noise and reached down to the bookcase at his side and pulled out a book on dinosaurs. "This'll keep your mind off things," he said. "Got your paper?"

I ran into the kitchen to ask for Gran for some greaseproof paper. I came back into the living room, where grandad was using his pen knife to sharpen the point of a pencil for me. I sat down at the dining table and carefully turned the pages of the book, marvelling at the diagrams and photographs of excavations, geological charts, and artists' impressions of the dinosaurs.

Most fascinating of all, were the painstakingly accurate ink drawings of the dinosaur skeletons. My favourite was the stegosaurus, instantly recognisable by the row of arrowhead shaped plates running along its spine. Every bone was depicted, even the tiny bone at the tip of the tail. I lay the sheet of greaseproof paper over the top of the illustration and stuck it in place with a piece of masking tape, which grandad had brought in from his workshop.

I began methodically tracing the lines, stopping every few minutes to sharpen my pencil with the grandad's penknife, in exactly the way he'd taught me. Once I had traced every line, I turned the sheet of paper over and holding the pencil at an angle, used the side of the lead to cover the area with a layer of graphite. Turning the paper back over I retraced the lines, transferring the graphite down on to a clean sheet of paper underneath. As I took away the sheet of greaseproof paper, there, in faint grey lines, appeared the skeleton.[7]

"How did the dinosaurs get so deep underground, Grandad?"

"Well, when they died, their bodies became covered in earth, layers and layers of it, over however many millions of years."

"How did they die?"

"Now there's a question." He turned a page and found a T-Rex.

"Maybe their bodies became too big for their brains. Some were the size of a walnut, you know."[8]

"I think Darren's brain might be even smaller than that," I said, causing Grandad to cough on the tea he'd just drunk. I held up my drawing of the stegosaurus skeleton, and Grandad gave me a thumbs up.

"Come September, you'll be doing art classes at secondary school. Bet you can't wait?" said Grandad, pouring himself another cup of tea from the pot.

---

[7] I still have the very same copy of *Men and Dinosaurs* by Edwin H. Colbert on my bookshelf today. If the pages are held to the light, it is possible to see the indentations made by my pencil as it traced the lines of the skeleton illustrations all those years ago.

[8] Grandad's theory on dinosaur extinction represented just one of the theories prevalent at that time. It wasn't until 1980 that father and son researchers Luis and Walter Alvarez put forward the claim that a massive asteroid had slammed into Earth, creating Chicxulub Crater on Mexico's Gulf Coast and causing the mass extinction.

"Hhhmm," I replied, "maybe."

"You don't sound so sure? What's bothering you lad?"

"Grandad, is it true that the big kids give the first year kids bog-washes?"

"What on earth is a bog-wash?"

"They stick your head down the toilet and pull the flush."

"Now whoever's been telling you that sort of nonsense? You pay no attention to them. Just think about all the new things you'll get to learn and all the new friends you're going to make. That's all that matters. Besides, you got your big brother to look out for you, isn't that right Nicholas?"

My brother had just come back from the kitchen and was standing in the doorway flexing his muscles and pulling a funny face.

"You see," said Grandad, laughing, "No one's going to mess with the Incredible Hulk there."

CHAPTER 7

THE OAK MOTHER'S GARDEN

It was Monday morning and I was standing with my back to the railway arch. I didn't dare to look up for fear there might be a figure staring down at me, as in the dream from a few days ago. I focused my attention on the pair of grey wagtails that were busy bobbing about their business at the edge of the stream nearby. The sky was overcast and for the first time in a while I wished I was wearing anything other than my usual summertime t-shirt and shorts. I looked down to the playground where a couple of teenagers were sitting on the swings, rocking gently while talking to each other. Out on the open patch of meadow, a man was throwing a tennis ball for his dog to chase and bring back, something it did with never-ending enthusiasm.

Thoughts began spinning around inside my head. Shapes and shadows, names and faces, a torn veil and an oak tree. Just then I heard a familiar voice.

"You made it then?"

There was Aislinn at the top of the embankment. I ran up the steps to meet her.

"I'm ready to do this," I said.

"Are you sure? You don't sound sure," said Aislinn. I thought of the restless nights and vivid dreams, the times I'd raced home panic-stricken having seen a flickering shadow moving towards me. I longed for the day when this would all stop.

"Yes, I'm sure."

"Come on then," said Aislinn and she grabbed my arm and started to run, dragging me along with her. As we sprinted along the old railway track I looked down the side of the embankment to the gas pipe where I'd first seen Aislinn. We sped past the rope swing that still hung down from the lofty branch and after a hundred metres or so we came to a small gap in the trees and bushes at the side of the track.

"Here it is," said Aislinn. "I marked the tree trunk, look." She pointed to the outline of a star that had been scratched into the bark. She stepped through the gap in the undergrowth and I followed. We were walking carefully down the steep slope of the embankment, a covering of branches and leaves above our heads.

"Careful, this is where I slipped," said Aislinn as we came to a short vertical drop. We sat on the ground and eased ourselves down, feet first until we reached the bottom of the slope. Here we met a wall of undergrowth and Aislinn began looking around for something on the ground.

"There it is," she said, kneeling down next to an empty paint tin. "I left it here as another marker, you see." I knelt down beside her and watched as she began crawling on her hands and knees into a hole in the undergrowth. I followed, wincing occasionally as the brambles scratched my bare arms. It was then that I felt an odd sensation, as if a wave of cold air had passed through my body.

We came out on the other side of the undergrowth and rather than arriving at City Bank allotments as I was expecting to, I found we were standing at the edge of a garden more beautiful than I could ever imagine. I had expected to see a vision straight out of my nightmares, a place of desolation dotted with blackened tree stumps and hissing pools of sulphur. Instead, here was a place of wonder where nature seemed to have re-invented itself, taking all its familiar designs and forms and switching them around slightly. Some plants seemed to be moving of their own accord and the birdsong sounded as though I was hearing it backwards. Everything around us was bathed in a soft violet light and the air was filled with a perfume so exquisite, I felt it couldn't be real.

"Welcome to the Otherlands," said Aislinn. I was staring wide eyed, my mouth falling open.

"We're here already?" I said turning my head in all directions, trying to take in as much of my surroundings as I possibly could. "My dad would love a garden like this, although he'd never keep it looking this amazing."

"Come on, let's see if the Oak Mother's at home."

I followed Aislinn through the garden, marvelling at the toadstools that stood tall as streetlamps and the pale flowers that seemed to almost glow like Christmas lights. Tree branches unfurled like long fingers as if they were reaching down to touch the tops of our heads.

We climbed a set of stone steps that led to a small area of lawn, at the end of which stood an oak tree. Its broad trunk, impossibly knotted and gnarled, stood squat beneath a maze of branches; limbs that had, over time, turned and twisted in every conceivable direction. From these limbs grew leaves, whose colour and soft lustre were like that of aged bronze. Set into the trunk of the tree was a small door. As Aislinn walked up to it, I could see that it was no taller than she was. She knocked on it loudly then beckoned me to join her but I kept my distance, not knowing quite what to expect.

After a while there came the sound of bolts being undone before the door swung inwards.

A round faced peered round the edge of the door. Small eyes sparkled beneath a mass of tousled grey hair. "How nice to see you, young lady." The voice was cracked and reedy. "You brought your friend I see."

She nodded in my direction.

"Yes, this is Steven. He's the one I told you about," said Aislinn.

"Ah yes, him that was talking to no one. Well you'd better come in then hadn't you," said the Oak Mother and she disappeared back inside the tree.

"Come on then," said Aislinn, "I told you she was nice."

Aislinn stooped slightly as she stepped through

the door and I did the same, taking care to close the door behind me without slamming it. Just inside the door, wooden steps led down through the roots of the tree, lit by a soft violet light coming from what looked like crystals set into the walls at various points. As my eyes adjusted, I saw that the ceilings were low, almost touching the tops of our heads but we were able to move about easily enough. The Oak Mother's home was a cavern divided into separate chambers, the first being the kitchen, with a fireplace built into the wall and a huge black pot hanging over the flames. There were two small wooden cupboards with a few baskets stacked on top, overflowing with spiral shaped carrots and spring onions.

We passed the next chamber which was crammed full of pots, jars and bottles containing all sorts of plants, powders and liquids. In the centre of the chamber there stood a square block of stone upon which was a large brass bowl.

"That's the potion room," said Aislinn, "I love to help mix the potions, although some of them smell quite bad." We turned a slight corner and walked through an archway and here is where we found the Oak Mother. She was sitting at a writing desk that looked to have been carved from a single piece of wood. The walls of this chamber were covered from floor to ceiling with shelf upon shelf of neatly stacked books.

"This is the library," said Aislinn, a smile spreading across her face.

I ran my fingers along the books, each of them beautifully bound in moss-coloured cloth; their titles embossed into the spines and written in a language I couldn't understand.

"What are all these books about?" I asked.

"Oh, there are books on plants and trees, animals, insects and birds, books about the weather, the landscape, the rocks and the rivers. There are books about foraging, medicine and cookery, books about languages, lettering and speech, and books containing stories, poems and songs as old as the sky. There are also books of spells and recipes for potions, some I've written myself, others passed down through the ages, their ingredients and methods unchanged since they first appeared however long ago. Everything I need to know is right here, in those books," said the Oak Mother proudly.

"What's this one here?" I said pointing to the book that was so large, it rested on the floor by itself. It was the biggest book I had ever seen. The spine was as long as my arm and as thick as my neck and it was bound in cloth the colour of conkers.

The Oak Mother gestured for me and Aislinn to help her lift the book up on to her desk. It was quite an effort but between the three of us we managed it. The book now lay open flat on top of the desk and the pages were bigger than those of my dad's Sunday newspaper. They were filled with beautiful handwriting, written in Christmas tree green ink. The Oak Mother began turning the pages.

"Look. Here's the story of Magpie Jack who steals things from people's homes. Doesn't matter what they are as long as they're small and shiny; anything from rings and coins to bottle tops and teaspoons. Any time something goes missing you can be sure it's the work of Magpie Jack."

I shuddered as I read the description of a man with a long black coat and a hat decorated with feathers, realising the figure I saw walking through the empty house on the building site that day would have been none other than Magpie Jack.

The Oak Mother turned to the next page. "Then there's Creeping Jenny, the girl that spends all her days up in the tree branches. Poisoned by ivy she was and never quite recovered. Oh, the trouble we have with her," said the Oak Mother tutting and shaking her head.

"Who writes the stories?" asked Aislinn.

"That's my responsibility," replied the Oak Mother.

"You've written all these stories?" gasped Aislinn, turning more and more pages. "There must be thousands and thousands."

"No, dear me," chuckled the Oak Mother, "I've not written all of them. Just those from the last couple of hundred years or so."

"You're two hundred years old?" I said.

"Thereabouts," replied the Oak Mother, straightening her back with some discomfort, "I've lost count to be honest."

"So who wrote them before you?" Aislinn asked,

"I'm not the only one of my kind you know. There have been many others before me. As one departs the next Oak Mother arrives. It's been that way since the beginning."

"It's like Doctor Who," I said.

"Doctor what?" asked the Oak Mother.

"Never mind," I said, once Aislinn and I had stopped giggling. "So the stories are about actual people?"

"No, not people," she replied, "Otherlanders. In here is the story of every single Otherlander that ever existed." I must have looked incredibly confused.

"Aislinn, you go make us a pot of mushroom tea while I talk with your friend here."

Aislinn cast me a questioning glance and I nodded to show I was happy for her to leave. The Oak Mother turned to face me.

"Aislinn tells me you've been having nightmares. She says you've seen things; figures and shadows."

I nodded my head.

"She's told you about the veil that separates our two worlds?"

I nodded once more.

"There are only a few children such as yourself – and Aislinn – who can see through this veil into our world. The figures you half-see in your dreams or out of the corner of your eye are the inhabitants of this world.

"I think Aislinn called them the Unseen?" I said.

"That's what you call them in your world. Here,

they're just Otherlanders."

"So they're real?" I said.

"As real as I am, sitting here next to you," replied the Oak Mother and she touched my shoulder to prove it.

"Where do they come from?" I asked. The Oak Mother looked at Aislinn who had reappeared in the doorway.

"You've not told him yet, have you?"

"No, Oak Mother, I haven't," replied Aislinn, "I thought it would be better coming from you."

"Told me about what?" I said, looking from Aislinn to the Oak Mother and back again.

"They come from here," said the Oak Mother and she gently pressed her finger against the side of my head. "The imagination. Home to such powerful energy. In some children, like you and Aislinn, this energy is even more powerful and fear feeds off it, growing and growing like an electrical storm. Eventually the storm has to break and it's in this explosion of energy that something incredible happens."

"What? What happens?" I asked, my fingers gripping the seat of the stool.

"The Unseen are born. Beings half-formed from your darkest thoughts. They begin wandering around, lost and trapped inside your imagination."

"If they're in my imagination, how come I can see them?"

"Because they want you to see them. They're calling to you, asking to be set free."

"To come here?" I asked.

"Yes, here in the Otherlands. This is where they become fully formed beings."

"How on earth do we set them free?" I asked,

"We extract them," said the Oak Mother. I winced at the thought of my head being sawn open and the Oak Mother using needles to pull the thoughts from my brain.

"Don't look so worried youngster," said the Oak Mother. "It's a completely painless process. In fact, it's quite spectacular."

"So you don't use a saw or a knife?" I asked.

"No of course not," said the Oak Mother laughing. "We use magic."

Aislinn sat cross legged on the floor next to me and we each took a sip from our mugs. The taste didn't seem to bother either of us as we sat transfixed, waiting for the Oak Mother to speak.

"What I need now, is for both of you to describe your visions of the Unseen. Are they short or tall, do they move quickly or slowly, or not at all? Whereabouts have you seen them? Tell me about the locations where they appear to you."

We took it in turns to talk. Aislinn described two tall bulky figures that would often lurch along the top of the embankment and the shadowy man that shuffled between the mill house and the pig sheds. I talked about the copse, where I'd catch sight of a blurred figure flickering and skipping about by the tin shack and the shape of a small woman sitting at the edge of the pond. I told her that they all had names and I'd made drawings of them.

"Then there's the silhouette of the little girl wandering through the culvert," said Aislinn,

"And the twisted thing that paces backwards and forwards outside the allotment shed," I added as I watched the Oak Mother writing notes on a piece of paper.

After a while, she put down her pen, which looked to have been made from a delicately sharpened twig.

"Well, that's all I need for now. You two better run back home and I can get on with writing these stories."

Aislinn and I walked out of the garden and headed towards the opening in the veil. I tried to imagine what stories the Oak Mother would attach to each of the Unseen. If she was right, these stories would be the foundations from which each character would develop and evolve, changing from half-formed monsters into fully formed beings. The Oak Mother's words were echoing inside my head.

"Remember, none of us get to choose how our story begins, it's the choices we make along the way that really count."

CHAPTER 8

STORIES OF THE UNSEEN

THE PIG MAN

No one knows his real name, he is known simply as the Pig Man. Ever since he was cursed by the Elm Witch, he has lived a solitary life in the big grey house built on the side of the river. He was once a perfectly normal person, who made a living restoring cars, trucks and aeroplanes in a workshop at the end of his garden.

The Elm Witch lived nearby, on the tiny island formed where the river split into two. She had grown tired of the noises coming from the busy workshop, the sound of engines firing and revving and the hammering and grinding of metal, day in day out. She was sick of the fumes and smoke being pumped into the air from the exhausts, and eventually she decided she'd had enough. One morning as the man walked through the garden to his workshop, the Elm Witch hid in the overhanging branches of an apple tree. As the man passed beneath her, she scattered a handful of petals down onto his head. The petals had been dipped in a potion and as they gently touched his face, a dramatic transformation was set in motion.

Over the next few days, he noticed a strange feeling about his face, as if his skin was being stretched. He looked in the mirror and he could clearly see that his nose had grown, and his nostrils were becoming wider. His ears too, seemed to be much bigger, and the tips had started to fold over.

A week later, his transformation was complete. His body, arms, legs, feet and hands had remained the same, but atop his shoulders, where the head of a ruggedly handsome man had once sat, was now the head of a pig. There was also an impressively curly tail which appeared exactly where you'd expect a tail to appear.

The Pig Man stopped working on his cars and aeroplanes, and shut himself away in the house. He lived in fear of human contact, aware that his changed appearance would give a great shock to any visitors.

"If I am to look like a pig," he said to himself as he looked in the mirror one morning, "then I am only fit for the company of pigs."

From that moment on he decided his role in life would be as a keeper of pigs. The Pig Man set about building a piggery on a piece of land not far from the house, using sheets of corrugated iron, old farm gates, assorted wooden doors and rusted car panels. He arranged for a local farmer to deliver a pair of Gloucester Old Spot pigs to him, which arrived a week later on a trailer pulled behind a rusty old machine that looked a bit like a tractor.

A few months later there was a whole family of pigs scuttling around inside the piggery, snaffling up the food brought to them by their devoted owner. The pigs were never sent for slaughter; the Pig Man raised them from piglets, and they lived in the piggery until they passed away naturally. He buried them on a strip of land next to the river, marking each one with a gravestone cut from a sheet of metal, the names and dates of the deceased written using an oxyacetylene torch.

The Pig Man still keeps himself hidden away and children will often dare each other to look in through the windows of the house, to catch a glimpse of him dressed in his long brown overcoat, tied up with an old kipper tie, and the wide brimmed hat from under which pokes his pink snout.

THE TROLLS

There is a network of rooms and passages dug out of the earth on one side of the railway embankment. This is where two adult trolls live. During the day they stay in their underground home, sleeping. At night they venture out into the small copse that spreads out from the bottom of the embankment, or head up onto the top, sticking to the lines of trees and undergrowth, where they can stay hidden from view. While out and about at night, the wood trolls gather wild garlic, mosses and cow parsley which they eat in large amounts. They are particularly fond of toadstools and poisonous berries despite the chronic stomach cramps they cause. In fact, the trolls find these side effects to be strangely pleasurable. They also feed on the rats and spiders found in the damp confines of the culvert. Occasionally, the trolls will venture as far as the cottages at the far end of the embankment, where they raid the compost heaps, picking out hunks of mouldy bread and onions whose skins have turned black.

On rare occasions, the wood trolls have been known to feast on children caught playing outside after dark.

THE LONELY CLOWN

At one time, the clown used to perform as part of a travelling circus. He was an incredible performer, with a natural ability to reduce any audience to a helpless mess of laughter. He wore an oversize coat, made from a crazed patchwork of scrap material, and from the pockets sewn inside, he would pull out all sorts of peculiar items; a group of sock puppets that could sing operatic arias, a pair of hobnail boots that took off from the ground and flew about the arena, whizzing above the audience, performing loop the loops and breath-taking death rolls. There was even a troupe of tap-dancing rubber chickens. No one knew his secrets, not even the other circus members, and with every performance the crowds marvelled as he somehow brought the objects to life.

The clown's one true love was Sophia, the elephant keeper. He watched as she tenderly worked with these enormous creatures and his heart glowed as he listened to her speaking to them as if they were her brothers and sisters. In Sophia's company, the elephants were playful and content. She was never strict with them, and she never forced them to do anything they didn't already want to do. She taught them to play football with each other and to perform dance routines together and everybody loved them.

One summer, when the circus arrived at City Bank, Sophia led the elephants to the stream, where they immediately began sucking water up into their trunks and spraying themselves, each other and Sophia, noisily trumpeting their delight.

The clown was helplessly in love with Sophia, but sadly for him, Sophia was in love with Alfredo, the trapeze artist. Alfredo performed with his brother Alonzo, and the pair of them were athletic, graceful and incredibly strong. The brothers would astonish audiences with seemingly impossible feats, and the clown would stand aghast as he watched from offstage. Sophia would throw her arms around Alfredo every time he'd arrive backstage after finishing his act. The relief that he had survived another death-defying performance only added to her love for him.

The clown realised that he could no longer live as part of the circus, as long as Sophia was there with Alfredo.

Late one night, as the rest of the troupe slept, he packed his coat and all his funny objects into a large sack, and headed over the embankment and into the copse. From then on he chose to live a life of solitude, in a shack he'd built from scrap left lying around the woods. He ate plants and drank from the stream. His only company were the birds in the trees, the hedgehogs that would come snuffling up to the doorway of his shack and the fox that wandered by on its nightly ramble. He would chatter away to his puppets, discussing the weather and what food they would eat and whereabouts in the woodland they would find it.

The rest of his time was spent time entertaining himself with juggling fir cones, or practising his tumbles on a mat of leaves and moss. These moments of contentment were short-lived and on the whole, his life was one of great sadness. Anyone who, by chance came within sight of the clown, was touched with an overwhelming sense of tragedy and loneliness.

THE OLD GREEN GRUMBLE

In a dilapidated shed, in a far corner of the North Home Road allotments, lives the Old Green Grumble. His days are mostly spent hidden away, in the cramped and dusty confines of his shed, drinking creosote and eating Brussels sprouts. His only companions are the woodlice, earwigs and mice that have taken up joint residence. At one time in his life, he worked as a farmhand, spending an unhealthy amount of time patrolling the land on the lookout for trespassers. It is said that over the years, many children had been chased off the property by a bony, bandy-legged figure, brandishing a shotgun.

On one particular occasion, a group of older youths had somehow managed to enter the farmyard, climb on board the farmer's tractor and start it up. They began driving haphazardly about the yard and it wasn't long before they crashed into the hay barn, creating untold damage and causing the chickens nesting there to die of shock. It had been the Old Green Grumble's responsibility to ensure that the tractor was safely locked away in the garage, but he'd been so pre-occupied with hunting trespassers that day that he'd clean forgotten to do so. The farmer had no choice but to give the Old Green Grumble his marching orders, and from that moment on, his hatred of children grew ever stronger.

THE SWAN LADY

As a child the Swan Lady lived a very tragic life. Her parents were not nice people, in fact they were terrible people who one day decided they wanted rid of her. She was barely two years old when her parents wrapped her in a blanket, placed her in a plastic washing up bowl and headed out into the countryside. They eventually came to a river and there they set down the bowl with the infant inside and pushed it out into the middle, where it was carried away by the current.

Who knows for how long she had been drifting before a pair of swans swam over to her, intrigued by the sight of this strange object. When the swans saw the baby inside, they set about pushing the bowl to the riverbank using their strong necks. When they reached the bank, the swans clasped the edge of the bowl in their bills and pulled it up on to the bank, where they waited for the rest of the day until a lady walking her dog happened to pass by. The lady gasped when she saw the infant, and immediately picked her up and hugged her, gently swaying her from side to side, uttering words of kindness and reassurance. She looked down at the swans and spoke to them.

"She'll be safe now, you two. I'll make sure she finds a home and that she's looked after, don't you worry." The swans bowed their heads before easing themselves back into the water and gliding away.

The Swan Lady did find a new home, and even though her adoptive family could not have been kinder or more loving, she was never able to trust humans ever again. Throughout the years, she dedicated her time and energy into building an animal sanctuary, in the copse behind the railway embankment. Here she kept the injured birds and small animals she rescued from parks, gardens, rivers and roadsides.

She built enclosures using willow branches and

bracken, and made sure they were spacious enough to allow the swans, ducks and geese to spread their wings fully, so that their muscles might be stretched and their feathers straightened. The enclosures are still there today, arranged in a circle, at the centre of which lies a pond, and here the birds get to take a paddle and socialise. The peacock looks on disapprovingly, horrified that any bird would allow their feathers to touch the muddy water.

At night the Swan Lady sits moon-bathing at the edge of the pond. She will often start singing a mournful song that could be mistaken for the call of a tawny owl. She still prefers the company of birds and animals to humans and has gone so far as to train an army of crows, who upon her command, will savagely attack any person or child found wandering too close to the sanctuary.

RAT KID

Two young girls dared each other to walk the length of the culvert, where the river ran from the meadow, through the embankment and out into the copse on the other side. They stood in the river, at the mouth of the tunnel, each waiting for the other to back out. The younger of the two, was the first to move. She took a few steps and began walking into the tunnel. Once they were both inside, they stared up at the roof, trying not to think of the vast amount of earth suspended above them. They walked further into the tunnel, keeping their eyes fixed on the opening at the far end, where daylight appeared more enticing than ever. The walls of the tunnel were slimy with moisture and the smell of damp was almost overpowering. They stood in the middle of the tunnel, shouting and singing, enjoying the sound as it echoed all around them.

Then the younger of the two girls let out a shriek and kicked at the water about her feet.

"Something bit me," she cried and started running towards the exit, water splashing all around her, drenching her shorts and t-shirt.

"Wait a minute. Don't leave me on my own," said her friend, running after her. At last they reached the opening at the far end. They climbed up on to the bank at sat down, panting and shivering, the younger girl holding her ankle. She took her hands away to reveal two lines of blood, running from puncture marks made by two very sharp front teeth.

"I told you there were rats in there," she said, tying her sock around the wound before setting off for home in floods of tears.

This wasn't just any old rat. It had been poisoned by the Elm Witch. She had grown tired of it sneaking into her hut at night to raid her food store. As punishment she had laced some bread with deadly wolfsbane, which the rat had proceeded to eat. Somehow, the rat survived the poisoning, but not without acquiring some curious biological changes.

Unfortunately, this was passed on to the girl through the bite and so days later, she started to notice changes in the structure of her face. Her nose was growing longer, as were her front teeth – and at either side of her mouth, whiskers had started to sprout. Soon her ears became much larger and stuck out from her head. Her appearance was soon so bizarre, that she refused to leave her room. Her mother had to slide food under her door and for days she lived off nothing but crackers and slices of cheese. She would drink water from the bathroom tap, but only when everyone else was asleep.

One morning, before anyone else was awake, she scuttled out of her house on Victoria Road and along the railway embankment until she came to the culvert. She dropped down into the river and waded into the tunnel. Before long, the water was alive with rats, their dark bodies hidden in the black water, only the pink of their claws and tails visible in the gloom. They had come as one, to welcome their new friend.

CHAPTER 9

MONK'S MOUND

That night, I hardly slept at all. My mind was filled with the sight of thorny brambles slithering under my bedroom door, of roots and creepers climbing up the bedposts, their tendrils coiling into my ears and nostrils. I imagined a seething mass of chucky pigs and earwigs beneath my mattress, and a steady rain of earth falling over my body as I lay helpless in my bed.

I was woken by my brother calling to me from downstairs.

"Do you want Coco Pops or Frosties?"

"I don't mind," I shouted back, checking to see if there was any dirt or leaves in my hair. Last night's dreams had been so vivid, my skin felt itchy, as if the creepy crawlies were still scuttling around inside my pyjamas.

"I'll leave you the Frosties then,"

"OK," I said before walking into the bathroom to run my head under the cold tap. As I was drying my hair, my brother came into the bathroom to brush his teeth.

"You were fidgeting in your sleep last night, you alright?" he said.

"Oh sorry, yeah, I fell in the stingers yesterday and it was itching like mad." I didn't dare tell him the truth, that I'd been anxious about today, when the Oak Mother was due to perform the extraction spell on me and Aislinn.

"Are you coming with us to Monk's Mound? Jensen said he found some chicken heads there."[9]

"I might join you later – I'm not feeling very well at the moment."

"Mum's packing us sandwiches, and some cans of Panda Shandy,"

"I've got a bit of a stomachache,"

"Fair enough. I'll save a can for you."

"Thanks Nick," I said, a little pathetically. "Try not to shake it up too much."

---

[9] Monk's Mound is the name given locally to the prehistoric round barrow located just north-east of Cirencester. It was first mentioned in AD 1200 as Thorebarewe, then later by William of Worcester in 1460 as Castrum Torre. It was also reported in Daniel Defoe's *A Tour Through The Whole Island of Great Britain* first published in 1724.

The area may well have been a prehistoric ritual precinct and was probably reused in early Roman times as the focal point for a cemetery and temple complex.

The barrow also featured in Arthurian legend. Some time between the 5th and 6th centuries, Caradog, Prince of Gwent and a Knight of the Round Table visited Cirencester (Caer Ceri) on royal business and upon walking outside the town walls he chanced upon the beautiful Tegau, who hailed from Cirencester. Tegau became his wife.

Nick's grin disappeared downstairs, and I heard the front door slam as he left the house to meet the rest of the gang who were waiting at the top of our garden steps. I peered out of the bathroom window, trying not to be seen. I saw Hewett and his brother Martin, the twins Leah and Sarah and Mental Jensen, each with carrier bags filled with sandwiches, crisps and cans of pop. Mental Jensen threw his chewing gum at Hewett and it stuck in his hair. Hewett grimaced as he pulled the gum free, taking a clump of hair with it.

Jensen was a troublesome kid, who made a habit of going one step too far. He was always fidgety and impatient, gnawing his fingernails and the skin around them until they were sore and bleeding. He shouted, rather than spoke, and was often involved in fights at school. He never talked about his parents, and no one had been to his house. Still, he was the most fearless kid I knew, and would always be the first to test a new rope swing, or walk all the way through the culvert on his own. He once jumped from the top of the stairs at Hewett's house, landing at the bottom without injuring himself.

Then there was the time we built a ramp, using a plank of wood and some breeze blocks we'd brought back from an abandoned building site. We'd set it up in the middle of the street, and being in a cul-de-sac there was little traffic, particularly during the week when parents were at work. A few of us were jumping over the ramp on our bikes, and already quite a large group of kids had gathered to watch.

It was then that Mental Jensen appeared on his brother's racing bike. He had set himself as far back along the street as possible to gain maximum speed upon reaching the ramp. There was a tangible sense of astonishment among the crowd at the speed with which he hit the ramp, and a second or two of total silence as the bike arced through the air before slamming back down on to the tarmac. The front wheel, taking all the impact, bent almost in half and the back wheel flipped up, sending Jensen out of the saddle and over the handlebars before he sprawled on to the road with a sickening crunch.

He stood up, brushed the grit and dust from the horrendous grazes on his arms and the palms of his hands, the left knee of his jeans was torn, and a nasty egg-shaped lump was rising on his temple. He was visibly shaken, but determined to prove he was not too bothered. He picked the bike up under one arm and hobbled off back towards his house, no doubt terrified about the reaction his brother was going to have.

"It was a rubbish bike anyway," he shouted back at us, and disappeared around the corner.

"We should go after him, check he's alright," said Michael, and seeing no one else step forward to volunteer, he marched off in the direction of Jensen's house.

"*Wait,* I said – we'll come with you." Hewett and I ran to catch up. We arrived at Jensen's front gate, which hung from one hinge, and squeaked loudly as we opened it. The front yard was littered with bin bags, broken plastic toys and an old mattress, and we stepped over a pile of dog muck before knocking on the front door. There were raised voices from inside, and we could see the distorted shape of someone in the rippled glass. The door opened and there was Jensen's mum.

"What's the matter boys?" she asked.

"We just wanted to check that Jens ... *Mark* is ok," said Michael.

"He's alright, a few scrapes and bruises. It's the bike that's come out of it worse."

"Can you tell him we asked about him, and we hope he gets better."

"Yeah, I'll tell him, right after I've sewn up the hole in his jeans."

"Okay, bye then. Sorry," said Michael and we shuffled off back to the ramp, where a car had stopped, waiting for the kids to clear the way. There was nothing more we could do.

Today, I watched as the gang set off along Golden Farm Road, on their trek to Monk's Mound. Once they were out of sight, I headed back to my room and read the first chapter of my new library book, *Dominic* by William Stieg. The story starts with Dominic, a restless inquisitive dog, deciding one day to leave his home in search of change. He pins a note to his front door, addressed to his friends, saying he doesn't know when he'll be back and apologising for not having time to say goodbye. At a fork in the road, he meets a witch alligator, who urges him to take the path on the left. This path, she assures him, leads to adventure and untold wonders.

It was time for me to go. Aislinn would be waiting for me at the entrance to the Otherlands.

CHAPTER 10

THE SPELL CHAMBER

I crawled out from the hole in the undergrowth and there was Aislinn, sitting on the ground beside the opening.

"You're here," she said excitedly, "Come on, the Oak Mother will be waiting."

I'd only just climbed to my feet when she took my arm and led me around the edge of the garden to where a blanket of creepers hung down from the top of a steep rock face. The leaves of the creepers were the colour of Parma Violets. Aislinn gently brushed them aside with her arm and walked through a hidden opening in the rock face. Nervous but determined, I followed her.

I found myself stepping into a large dome shaped chamber, whose walls were decorated with leaf patterns carved directly into the rock. There were small recesses placed at regular intervals around the circumference of the cave. From out of these recesses came the most extraordinary coloured glow – like Turkish delight. As my eyes adjusted, I could see a crystal the size of an ostrich egg set inside each recess, from which the light gently pulsed. In the centre of the cave stood a plinth. It cradled a large book. Standing at the plinth was the Oak Mother. She smiled as Aislinn and I joined her.

"Come and look," said the Oak Mother and she invited us to stand either side of her. The book was covered in what looked like the softest, smoothest moss that ever existed. The edges were trimmed with thin twigs that had been curved and shaped to form impossibly intricate designs. Aislinn slowly lifted the front cover to reveal the inside of the book, and there on the first page, in the same Christmas tree green ink, were eight neat lines of writing.

"What does it say?" asked Aislinn. The Oak Mother cleared her throat and began to read aloud:

When shadows take form and climb out of the silence,
When that which once lay hidden now crawls into view,
Here is the time to take heed.
For these are the Unseen, born of fear,
Their presence a reminder
Of darkness and danger.
Grant them life, that they may find their home,
And here shall they be met ... in the Otherlands.

The Oak Mother turned to the next page and there was a map of the Otherlands. My eye wandered across the page, following the path of the river as it wound its way through the copse and along the edge of the meadow. There was the embankment, rising out of the landscape like the spine of a sleeping dragon. The other locations and landmarks were there too; every detail captured through a delicate use of line – the Wood Trolls' den, the Pig Man's house, the Swan Lady's pond and the Elm Witch's island. It truly was a work of art.

The next pages were filled with drawings of the Unseen; the Pig Man in his wide-brimmed hat, the Clown in his patchwork coat and the Swan Lady surrounded by her crows. They overlapped and repeated themselves to the point that the drawings almost appeared to be moving, just like cartoons. The faces seemed to form different expressions, and I could almost hear sounds coming from their mouths – as if they were actually talking, or grunting or whatever they did to communicate. The figures appeared to be walking, dancing, crawling, hobbling and squatting, all within the boundaries of a page.

"What do those words mean?" I said, pointing to the lines of lettering that accompanied the drawings.

"They are the origin stories of the Unseen, and below that are the incantations and spells we'll use to bring *your* stories to life! Now, if you are both ready, we can begin."

I looked at Aislinn and she looked at me.

"I'm ready," said Aislinn.

"Me too," I said. Both of us were trembling.

The Oak Mother walked with us to the centre of the chamber where a mat weaved from long slender leaves had been laid on the floor. She invited us to sit and make ourselves comfortable.

"Just remember, you have to be completely silent throughout the spell casting," said the Oak Mother. "My words must be heard clearly otherwise the extraction spell won't work."

I mimed zipping my mouth shut and Aislinn giggled. The Oak Mother returned to the plinth where she stood for a moment with her eyes closed. She breathed slowly and deeply three times and began reciting from the book.

I had no idea what those words meant, but as she spoke it was like hearing the colour of starlight. The words danced like raindrops falling on a forest canopy. Slowly the pale violet glow inside the chamber began to grow stronger and I felt a tingling sensation moving across the top of my skull. I looked up to see a thousand multi-coloured sparks flickering and dancing in the air above our heads. Aislinn and I watched, mesmerised as the sparks came together to form clusters, like galaxies.

Even if I had been able to say something at this moment, my words would have been futile, as nothing could rival what I was experiencing. The clusters of light were now forming liquid shapes, pulsing and stretching, changing into what looked like figures, or beings. Aislinn and I began pointing up at them. Isn't that the Swan Lady? Look, it's the Pig Man! That looks like The Old Green Grumble, and there look, there are the Wood Trolls and Rat Kid!

All this time, the Oak Mother's words had been

transforming into a cacophony that sang out like a rain storm opening above our heads. I felt nothing beneath me, as if I were treading water in the deepest of oceans. One by one the figures of light drifted out of the cave, like dandelion clocks on a summer breeze. Then silence.

The Oak Mother breathed out slowly, and steadied herself against the plinth. She dropped her head slightly and held still for a few seconds. Her shoulders began to rise steadily as she breathed in and lifted her gaze to the ceiling. She sang a single note of purest tone, as if the moon itself had a voice. She paused, and then spoke.

"That is that," she said briskly. I'd been holding my breath most of this time. I noticed that Aislinn was touching the sides of her head, just as I was, as if making sure everything was still intact.

"Are you really sure it's all done?" I asked the Oak Mother as Aislinn and I slowly got to our feet.

"Yes, the extraction spell worked perfectly. The Unseen have been set free."

"Where are they now?" asked Aislinn.

"Somewhere between here and there, drifting blissfully in their half-formed state, waiting for the new dawn to arrive, when the light of the morning sun will bring them fully to life," The Oak Mother carefully closed the book and covered it with a large piece of dark red cloth.

As we stepped out of the chamber, I realised I had lost track of time. It could have been early evening. The Barley Sugar sun hovered just above the tree tops and a gentle breeze whispered its secrets between the branches.

"You two had better go home now and get some rest," said the Oak Mother.

"I don't feel tired at all," I said.

"Me neither said Aislinn, "In fact I feel as though I'm floating."

"Well you'll need to stay bright and alert, ready for your next visit," said the Oak Mother. "That's when you'll meet your creations."

Aislinn and I looked at each other, wide-eyed with the realisation that everything we'd always believed to be possible was about to change.

CHAPTER 11

A DISRUPTION

Deep underground, words were being spoken by a creature whose name those living above dared not utter. The name itself conjured images of yellow eyes blinking in the soil, of roots writhing like dying serpents, mouths lined with razor edged stones and limbs covered in thorns, claws clicking and twitching. For there, deep below the Otherlands were the Underlands, a world of caves, tunnels and holes where terrible beings lived terrible lives. They were ruled by the most terrible being of all, who went by the name of Bowelcreep, the Disruptor.

"I'm bored," growled Bowelcreep, as he slumped in a throne carved from a single block of quartz. He was a creature with long thick arms and hunched shoulders, and short stumpy legs that ended in wide flat feet with toenails that curled towards the ground. His body was bulky and misshapen, like a huge sack of potatoes with a lumpen clod of a head. A bulbous nose grew out over his broad, fat-lipped mouth. "Bored, bored, bored, bored, bored. Tell me Gryke, what is there to do in this rot hole?"

His second in command fussed about him, using a lump of chalk to scratch down a list on a piece of slate. "Well, it has been a while since we created a sinkhole?"

"Too much effort," yawned Bowlecreep.

"We could look for some more fossils to add to your collection?"

"There's nowhere to put them."

"Well then, how about we have a tidy up and a clearout?" suggested Gryke.

"Boring!" groaned Bowelcreep, his eyes following the course of a large black millipede that was scurrying across the floor towards him. It came up to his foot and tested the coarse wrinkled skin with its antennae. Bowelcreep raised his foot and brought it down gently on top of the millepede, trapping the creature beneath it. Bowelcreep looked down impassively as it struggled to break free. With a sharp twist of his foot, the millipede was wrenched in two, a wet crunching sound echoing around the chamber.

"Gryke, it's time we paid those Toplanders a visit," said Bowelcreep, his face splitting into a smile sour enough to curdle milk.

CHAPTER 12

CREEPING JENNY

Newly arrived in the Otherlands, my eyes were still adjusting to the strange light when the crows swooped down from the sky. I could hear the whistling of their feathers as they passed over my head. I watched warily as they dispersed into the tree branches close by. They cackled to one another, and I could hardly bare to imagine what they were saying about me. Just then Aislinn came crawling through the gap.

"You're here," I said with a sigh of relief. Aislinn jumped to her feet and looked around her.

"Come on, let's find the Oak Mother," she said, and we ran full speed across the garden towards the spell chamber. Once inside we looked around, expecting to find the Oak Mother, but there was no sign of her. I walked over to the book plinth on top of which was a folded piece of paper. It opened out into a map of the Otherlands, an exact copy of the one contained in the spell book. There was a small note attached to the map, written in the Oak Mother's familiar handwriting.

Come and find me, I'll be waiting by the footbridge in the meadow.

"It's a test, isn't it," said Aislinn, "To see how brave we can be."

Immediately, a feeling of dread coursed through my body.

Were we really expected to walk out into the Otherlands by ourselves? The crows had already made their presence known and my mind was now reeling, thinking what else might be out there. Above all, I knew I must come face to face with my creations.

I was moving my weight from foot to foot, breathing rapidly, telling myself over and over that this was my chance, to finally rid myself of this fear. If it meant I would sleep easily, without cowering under the bedclothes, bursting to pee, because I was too scared to get up in the night and go to the toilet, then it was worth it. If it meant I could walk home from school without fear of being followed by a mysterious figure, half-human, half-goodness knows what, then surely I should see this through.

I lay the map out flat on the plinth and my eyes darted about figuring out where each location was in relation to the others.

"Here we are," I said pointing to the drawing of the spell chamber on the map, "and here is the footbridge. It isn't far, we just have to go through this woodland

and we're there." I folded the map back up and help on to it tightly. I noticed that Aislinn was biting her nails. This was the first time I'd seen her show any signs of anxiety. I realised she'd been holding herself together up until this point and she was just the same as me.

"I've never been beyond the garden," she said. "I feel safe here."

"I'm going to count to three and then we go. Okay?" and without waiting for Aislinn to reply, I began counting loudly.

"One ... two ... three."

We burst out of the cave and turned on to the pathway that ran along the edge of the garden. The path was flanked on one side by a steep grassy bank where a line of standing stones loomed over us. The cracked and fissured surfaces of the stones had the craggy features of faces, their thick set eyes following our every move. I looked away, focusing my attention on the path up ahead of us where it disappeared into an area of woodland. The trees grew at awkward angles and the branches were sharp and bony like bird claws. As if reading each other's mind, we slowed down. Adder's tongue ferns hissed at our ankles and warted puffballs blew disapproving raspberries as we came to a halt.

"Do we have to go through there?" said Aislinn, catching her breath.

"According to the map, this is the only way to the footbridge," I replied.

"I bet that's where Creeping Jenny lives, the girl who

was poisoned by ivy. I bet she's in there somewhere,"

"Where *are* all the Otherlanders?" I said, looking around nervously.

"I think they're hiding," whispered Aislinn. "Probably watching us."

We looked at each other for a moment. Then, without prompting, we both started counting. One … two … three …

We took off again, racing through the trees, heads down, hearts thumping. We could hear the sound of mournful song drifting up from the beds of Monkshood that carpeted the forest floor. There were other sounds too, the rustling of leaves as something moved through the branches overhead, and a voice whispering to us.

The light had become quite dim now that we had reached the densest part of the woods and we carried on running until something stopped us in our tracks. Crouching on a high branch a few metres ahead of us, we saw the shape of a girl, her clothes covered in bindweed and twigs, her glowing green eyes staring down.

"It's her," whispered Aislinn, "It's Creeping Ivy."

"We should run." I said, readying myself.

"Or we could try talking to her?" said Aislinn.

"What if she doesn't want to talk to us?"

"We have to at least try," said Aislinn, "Then she'll know we are not a threat."

Although Aislinn's words made sense, I wasn't ready to hear them. In a moment of mad panic I started running towards the silhouetted figure and as I did so I let forth a loud continuous wail. Clearly startled, the girl scrambled up the tree and disappeared into the higher branches. I carried on running and I could hear Aislinn calling to me as she tried to catch up. I saw an opening in the trees up ahead and I picked up speed, desperate to be clear of the woods.

The path ended at a set of steps that took me onto the bridge and as soon as my feet touched the wooden boards I felt an immense sense of relief. I stood on the bridge with my arms hanging down over the side. I looked into the stream, the water reflecting the pale violet colour of the sky, and I waited for my breathing to slow to a normal rate.

"You made it then," said the Oak Mother from the other end of the bridge. I was so happy to see her, I had to stop myself from running over and throwing my arms around her. Just then Aislinn stepped up on to the bridge and stood for a minute or so, breathing deeply, her shoulders heaving up and down.

"What happened, why did you run off like that?" said Aislinn.

"I panicked. I thought she might attack us," I replied.

"You left me, I was on my own."

I hung my head in shame.

"It's only natural that you would panic," said the Oak Mother. "This world is unfamiliar to you and it is full of strangers. But remember, you are strangers to them. They will be scared too."

"I'm such an idiot," I admitted as a heavy wave of disappointment seemed to almost pull me to the ground.

"You're not an idiot," said Aislinn, nudging me and offering a smile in forgiveness.

"You're at the start of a journey and you've had a little stumble that's all," said the Oak Mother and she beckoned us to follow her over the bridge and on into the meadow. The sun was peering down through scattered clouds that seemed to curl and coil their way across the sky. The grass brushed against my bare legs as we walked in the direction of the embankment.

"Just on the other side is the copse, that's where you'll find the Lonely Clown," said the Oak Mother pointing at the steep ridge of earth that loomed across the top of the meadow.

"Does he live in a tin shack like the one in my world?" I asked.

"Why don't you go see for yourself?" said the Oak Mother.

"Now, you mean?" I said, panic setting in once again.

"Of course, the sooner you confront him, the sooner you'll overcome your fear. You two can go together – only as far as the edge of the copse, mind. Then Steven will have to meet the clown by himself. That's the way it's done. Aislinn will need to meet her creations too."

The Oak Mother sat down, her short legs jutting

out over the edge of the riverbank. "I'll be right here," she said and started humming a wistful tune.

CHAPTER 13

FIRST ENCOUNTERS

With some trepidation, Aislinn and I headed along the track that skirted one edge of the copse. Through the fan-shaped ferns and contorted hornbeam trees we caught sight of the Lonely Clown's shack. It was a simple structure made of corrugated metal sheets attached to wooden uprights. Poking out of the roof, we saw a metal chimney pipe, from which a thin trail of smoke coiled up into the overhanging tree branches.

"He must be at home then," said Aislinn.

"I wonder what he's cooking in there." I was trying hard not to think what it might be.

"I have to wait here remember," said Aislinn looking at me rather apologetically.

My breathing quickened as I set off along the thin path that wound its way through the undergrowth. I took one last look back at Aislinn over my shoulder and pressed forward until I was only a few metres away from the shack.

Suddenly the clown appeared from the doorway. I

ducked down behind a fern, which was shaped rather like a large coiled pencil sharpening. It instantly spiralled in on itself, disappearing into the earth. I threw myself flat on the ground, hoping that I hadn't been seen. I lifted my head up just enough to peer at the clown. My luck was in. He was standing with his face turned up to the sky, breathing in deeply. He started taking off his long patchwork coat which he folded and lay gently on the ground.

He was wearing his baggy yellow and green checked suit and his oversize boots, which were white with red toe caps. I noticed there was a small wind-up gramophone on the ground next to him, and as I watched, he picked out a record from a wooden crate and placed it on the turntable. He gently moved the tone arm into position and after a few seconds of crackling noises, some dramatic piano music started playing out of the gramophone horn.

The clown began hopping from foot to foot, jabbing and swiping at thin air. It took me a little while to realise he was rehearsing one of his famous routines, in which he boxed an imaginary opponent. He grunted and puffed as he threw lightning quick punches while all the time he was bobbing and ducking, dodging the punches of his invisible opponent. He started skipping and prancing about the floor, dropping his arms to his side, goading his opponent in a provocative display of showmanship.

He soon paid the price for this tomfoolery when his

opponent clocked him squarely on the chin with an invisible sucker-punch. The clown threw himself into the air before landing spreadeagled on his back. He lay there, eyes closed, tongue hanging out of his mouth and I was sure I could hear the sounds of little cartoon birds flittering and tweeting above his head.

In my excitement I completely forgot myself and stood up from my hiding place. I began clapping my hands.

"Bravo!" I said. "Bravo!"

The clown lifted his head and looked at me, a stunned expression on his face. He quickly scrabbled to his feet and headed back towards the shack.

"Please don't go," I said, "I only want to talk to you."

He stopped in the doorway and stood with his head bowed, looking down at the ground.

"I just wanted to ask you something," I said, my voice shaking nervously.

The clown kept his head down, but beckoned me to follow him into his home. After some hesitation, I stepped inside.

The shack was no bigger than my bedroom. From the light of a few candles scattered about the space, I could make out the posters adorning the walls. They featured beautiful illustrations of circus acts, their names printed in ornate letters – *Diablo the Fire Breather, Mazelle the Lion Tamer, Giorgio the Knife Thrower*. And there, in one corner, was the poster for *Corky the Clown,* wearing his patchwork coat and ridiculous shoes. I spotted the troupe of rubber chickens, lined up against the wall, each wearing their tiny pair of tap shoes.

Pride of place, in the centre of the largest of the four walls was a poster bearing the title *Sophia and her Graceful Giants*. Dressed in a suave black tailcoat and top hat, the figure of Sophia was seen striking a dramatic pose, her white-gloved hands outstretched, one leg kicking high above her head. She was flanked either side by six magnificent elephants standing on their hind legs, curving their trunks up towards the roof of the big top.

The clown, still with his back to me, pointed to an old car seat next to an upturned milk crate that served as a table. I sat down and cleared my throat.

"I love these posters," I said, "the drawings are brilliant."

The clown walked over to the table carrying an old metal watering can, from which he poured steaming liquid into each of the tin mugs he'd placed in front of us. The liquid was the colour of weak Ribena. I looked at him and smiled, and for an instant he smiled back at me. In that moment, the sadness left his face, and in a very soft voice, he spoke.

"Rosehip tea? Water's fresh out the stream this morning."

I politely took a sip, and thankfully it didn't taste half as bad as I thought it would. I decided to get straight to the point of my visit.

"I was wondering if you'd like to do a show one day," I said, "for all the others here."

"Oh I don't do that anymore," he replied, staring at the steam rising from his mug.

"But I've seen you rehearsing, you're brilliant. You're so funny," I insisted.

"Well, I've not performed in front of an audience for years now, not since …" His voice trailed off and he started fussing about, stirring the tea in the watering can with the handle of an old paintbrush.

Just then, the Swan Lady appeared at the door. She was clearly shocked to see me, a human child, sitting at the table with a cup of rosehip tea in my hand, and she looked to the old clown with a questioning expression on her face. The clown shrugged his shoulders and looked down at the table.

"I need a hand fixing one of the enclosures," she said, rather abruptly "Looks like a scutterfuzz has gnawed its way through the bindings."

"Of course," I said, "I'd love to help."

"I was talking to Cork—" The Swan Lady stopped herself in mid-sentence. Her silvery-grey eyes turned to me. "Well just be careful you don't frighten my birds, they're injured you see."

"Absolutely, I will be very careful."

"Very well then, we'd better make a start," she said and disappeared from the doorway.

The clown and I walked the short distance from

his shack to the Swan Lady's sanctuary. I noticed the crows scattered about in the branches of a nearby tree, keeping their watchful eyes fixed on my every move.

The three of us spent a couple of hours stripping the bark from willow branches to make lengths of twine, which we then used to repair the damaged panels of the enclosure.

"This reminds of the time I helped my dad fix the hole in our garden fence. My brother and I had been playing football and I kicked the ball way too hard. It went straight through." I stopped, realising the others wouldn't understand what I was talking about.

Once we'd finished, the Swan Lady stood up and walked over to her hut. After a minute or so she returned carrying a peacock feather which she placed on the ground at my feet.

"For me?" I said, astonished.

She nodded her head, and walked back to her wooden hut.

"Thank you, thank you so much," I said, as one by one the crows left their perches and headed off towards the meadow, where they would pick the ground for earthworms and little black beetles.

CHAPTER 14

THE STRANGE VAN

The siren repeated its four note jingle, heralding the arrival of the mobile shop. Known in our house as *the Strange van* because of its owner being Peter Strange, this converted Leyland-lorry-come-travelling-corner-shop would visit housing estates all over the Cirencester area and out into the surrounding villages too.[10] Customers would flock to where the van had parked, and after climbing up the steps to gain entrance, they were greeted with shelf upon shelf of household goods; cleaning liquids and powders, light bulbs, toilet rolls, bags of flour and packets of dusters and J-Cloths. There were tins of every imaginable food item; custard, carrots, evaporated milk, black treacle and Spam, all stacked neatly behind the thin metal bars attached to the front of the shelves to prevent them from falling as the van turned a sharp corner.

---

[10] Peter Strange and his mobile grocery service were more commonly known in the area as the Beep Beep Man/ Van because of the sound made by the van's siren. For some reason, this was not the case in our house.

It was huge inside – TARDIS-like. I passed the meat counter, and couldn't help looking at the plate of chitterlings. Cold grey and greasy, it looked as if the animal had been opened up then and there, its intestines coiling onto the plate and left to ferment in their own juice. Pride of place on the counter stood the bacon slicer, its huge gleaming blade, spotless as ever, eager to ease its way through the pinkish grey leg of ham hanging nearby. I winced as I pictured Mr Strange's fingers moving within a whisker of its deadly edge.

I quickly moved along the walkway that ran the length of the van, separated from Mr Strange's side of the shop by the long glass fronted counter. As each customer called out the items on their list, Mr Strange walked back and forth, picking them from the shelves. This often involved climbing a wooden stepladder to reach the products stored either on the higher shelves or hanging from the ceiling.

On the counter at the far end of the van, was the wooden sweet tray and this was where kids from all over the area made their weekly pilgrimage. I stood on tiptoe, fingers clutching the top of the glass counter, peering over the edge of the tray, feasting my eyes upon the wonders before me. White Chocolate Fish and Chips, Aniseed Balls, Liqourice Sticks, Liquorice Comfits, Liquorice Wheels, Jelly Cherries, Jelly Snakes, Jelly Rings, Fizzy Cola Bottles, Cola Cubes, Bazooka Bubble Gum, Bubbly Bubble Gum, Foam Bananas, Cherry Lips, Flying Saucers, Fried Eggs, Mallow

Twists, Midget Gems and Milk Teeth. It was almost overwhelming. I would have to focus hard if I was going to make the best use of my five pence piece, but it was hard with the conversations taking place around me.

"Your Brian's skittles team done alright, dint'ney? Nice picture in the Standard."

"Yep, another blumin' trophy for me to dust."

"Din't see you down the Golden Farm last Friday, you missed a bit o' argy bargy."

"I 'eard all about it. Silly lot. If them blokes can't 'old their beer, they shouldn't go out drinkin."

"Well, I wouldn't stop mine goin' out. Rather that than him sat at 'ome mopin."

"Ere, you sin the state o' them new 'ouses? Covered in mud they is. That's kids what done that. I seen 'em, lobbing mud bombs. They'll break a window soon enough. I tell you, if they was my kids I'd 'ave their guts for garters." (My mind flashed to the plate of chitterlings). I tucked my head down between my shoulders, and dared not look up, for fear of drawing attention to myself.

"Well if my Tony ever caught 'em at it, God 'elp 'em."

I cringed even deeper, waiting as Mr Strange dropped some apples in to a brown paper bag. Holding it by the top corners, he sealed the bag with a few rapid twists. "Is that everything?"

"No, I've a few more things to get so you serve that young man up there first."

I panicked. I knew I had to make my choice quickly as I didn't want to test Mr Strange's patience. He'd already picked off one of the pink and white striped paper bags that were strung upon a hook, and held it open. I knew not to pick the sweets out myself, Mr Strange was insistent that only he could touch them, in the interests of hygiene, of course.

"Two Fruit Salads, two Black Jacks and a Candy Shrimp please."

"That'll be five pence then young man." I handed him the coin, thanked him and made my way along the passage to the front of the van, keeping my head down as I passed Mrs Caine on the way. I felt her suspicious gaze follow me, knowing that in her mind every child was a potential culprit responsible for defacing the new houses.

I was relieved to have escaped without trouble, and once out of sight of the van, I could finally appreciate my choice of sweets.

I ate the Candy Shrimp first, knowing that it would last only a few seconds, its spongy chewiness giving way to that sweet strawberry flavour as it dissolved in my mouth. Next, I plumped for a Fruit Salad, and after working it between my teeth for a few moments I started to receive the soft tang of pineapple. Was that banana too, hidden behind the subtle hint of peaches? It tasted of colour, with waves of sunny yellow and warm peach moving around my mouth and behind my eyes.

By the time I reached home I was working my way

through a Black Jack, the bitterness of the liquorice in stark contrast to the sweetness of the Fruit Salad. I walked down the steps to my front door, and found mum in the garden, straining to pull up a long-dead plant that now resembled a tentacled sea creature, washed ashore and baked by an unforgiving sun.

"Oh hello lovely boy. Did you get the things on my list?" she asked. I paused mid-chew, my face frozen in a look of horror.

"I take it that means no?" I looked down at the stripy paper bag containing the single remaining Black Jack, and hid it behind my back. As I stood there, the Strange van hurtled past, on the way to its next stop over in the new Beeches estate. There was no way I could catch it now.

"Sorry Mum," I said, pouting slightly, my bottom lip stained jet black.

"Right then, in that case *you* can have a go at getting this monstrosity up while I go in to town."

She handed me the garden fork and headed back into the house. I pushed the fork prongs into the ground and pulled back on the handle. There was a creaking sound as the roots strained, holding fast to their place in the earth. I'm not sure why, but at that moment I looked up and peered over the fence, towards the hawthorn tunnel. There stood a large black dog staring back at me with bright red eyes. We stayed staring at each other for a few moments before the dog turned and disappeared into the tunnel. I frantically ran back into the house, slamming the front door behind me. Mum was in the kitchen writing a shopping list. I tore past her, ran upstairs and locked myself in the bathroom.

"Are you alright lovey?" came Mum's voice from the bottom of the stairs.

"Yes, I'm fine, just desperate for the loo," I said breathlessly, sitting on the edge of the bath, waiting for my heartbeat to settle down. I thought I should be honest with Mum, tell her what I'd seen, but I knew she'd worry, be convinced I was having hallucinations. So I decided I would have to keep it to myself.

All the while though, I couldn't help thinking it was an omen and something awful was about to happen.

CHAPTER 15

NEW ACQUAINTANCES

Aislinn and I stood at the top of the culvert opening with our toes poking over the edge, looking down out our reflections in the water far below us. Aislinn was about to meet the first of her creations and in the short time I had known her, this was the quietest she had been.

We walked along the top of the opening and down the track that led to the riverbank. We were now standing at the side of the tunnel mouth and leaning forward, we peered inside. Light was reflecting off the water to form writhing patterns on the ceiling, like hundreds of electric eels frantically climbing over each other.

"I'll hide in these bushes," I said, crouching down behind a nearby plant. It looked like a type of succulent, with clusters of fleshy leaves that seemed to be waving at me like pudgy green hands. I heard Aislinn clearing her throat and calling into the tunnel.

"Hello, my name is Aislinnn. Are you there?" No reply, just the dripping of moisture from the ceiling, and the gentle babble of the stream as it flowed into the darkness.

"Hello, are you there Rat Kid? I just wanted to introduce myself," she said, a little louder this time. Just then, a silhouette emerged from the wall halfway along the tunnel. I could see the ears protruding from the sides of its head. As the figure neared the tunnel opening, its full form was revealed in the daylight. It was a young girl, dressed in dungarees and a lemon yellow t-shirt. As she lifted each foot out of the water I could see she was wearing a pair of white Dunlop daps. Her brown hair was bobbed, and through it poked her pale pink ears. She raised her head and looked at me with curious hazel-brown eyes, her nose and whiskers twitching, taking in my scent.

"It's very nice to meet you," said Aislinn, after a while, "I hope I haven't disturbed you." The girl looked away for a second, and instinctively scratched behind her left ear. She turned back to Aislinn and spoke in a quiet voice.

"Are you the creator?" she said.

Aislinn was clearly caught off guard as she didn't respond immediately. This was the first time either of us had been referred to in this way and here she was, confronted by a being born of her own imagination.

"I suppose I am," said Aislinn.

"Is this my home?" she said, looking around her.

"Yes, this is your home and the Pig Man, the Swan Lady the Oak Mother and me, we are all your family."

The girl held her face up to the sun and closed her eyes. A small smile came to the corners of her mouth, then all of a sudden she turned and walked back into the tunnel. I watched as her silhouette moved further away, before she turned and disappeared back into her hole in the tunnel wall.

I soon found myself walking along the path that would take me to the Pig Man's house. The river was flowing lazily beside me, its surface disturbed every now and again by a sudden flap of a tail and the flash of shiny scales. I started to imagine what beasts might be lurking under the water here in the Otherlands. Not a minnow or a trout; something half human, half crayfish, with pincers sharp enough to tear flesh from a child's leg.

Just then, the Pig Man's house came into view, rising out of the piles of scrap metal and vehicle parts surrounding it. The windows facing the river were covered with sacking. There was a door in the centre of the facade, and a short path led down to the decking that jutted out from the riverbank. In the short strip of lawn stood a light aeroplane with only one wing. I turned the corner, where an old fire engine was parked next to a tractor and a milk-float, all in various stages of repair and disrepair. I suddenly heard a commotion coming from around the next bend.

I ran as fast as I could towards the sound and there

lolloping towards me, came a huge pink sow, her ears flapping and her trotters clomping on the dried earth.

As soon as she saw me she stopped, looking this way and that way, hoping for a clue as to where she should go next. Instinctively, I spread my arms wide to bar her path and walked slowly towards her. She sniffed and huffed and shook her head so that her ears made a wonderful slapping noise. As she turned to walk the other way, there was the Pig Man, crouching down on one knee, holding out his hand. The sow gave her tail a wiggle and let out a couple of soft grunts, before toddling back towards her master. For a moment the Pig Man and I stood in silence, facing each other across a distance of ten feet or so.

He turned and walked back with the pig, to a part of the shed wall where the metal had been bent outwards. Evidently here was the means of escape for the adventurous sow. He ushered her back through the gap before tapping in a few nails to secure the metal sheet back into place. He looked towards me and raised his hand to tip the rim of his hat, in a gesture of gratitude. I smiled and waved back at him and he replied with a couple of quiet grunts.

Sometime later I was walking across the allotments towards the shed owned by the Old Green Grumble. I was all too aware of his fearsome reputation and I'd been toying with the idea of turning back and heading for home. However, I had made a promise to help these Otherlanders settle in, and I was determined to see it through.

The allotment in my home world was the usual network of plots and accompanying sheds, each testament to the personality of their owner. Some were immaculate with plots divided into neat sections and each plant carefully labelled. There were deftly constructed bamboo trellises supporting prize-winning runner beans and the fondant-like flowers of sweet peas. Rows of onion stalks stood proud like soldiers on parade, and emerald green feathery carrot tops leapt out at the eye against the rich chocolate brown of the expertly tilled soil. Others were a little less well maintained, and improvisation was clearly key. There were benches made from planks balanced upon milk crates, and a variety of homemade scarecrows scattered about the place, carrying out their work with varying degrees of success. Greenhouses displayed their patchwork of make-do repairs; broken panes replaced with offcuts of wood, pieces of cardboard or carrier bags taped to the frames. The sound of sport commentaries and weather forecasts crackled out of a multitude of transistor radios.

Here in the Otherlands the allotment was very different. Instead of sheds there were crazily constructed wooden cabins, with steep sloping roofs some of which were covered in spongy moss, others with thatch. Some cabins consisted of two storeys, with their upper levels propped up on rough hewn stilts and all the doors and windows were set at oblique angles. Plots were connected via a network of stepping stone pathways and everywhere, plants grew in abundance. There was something resembling rhubarb, its dark candy-striped stalks supporting leaves that were intricately webbed like a sea-fan coral. There were long slender pods hanging from spindly wooden trellis that coiled and uncoiled like watch springs and snapdragons that nipped at my ankles as I passed them.

I spotted several figures at work about the site, tending to the earth or loading up wheelbarrows filled with spiral shaped leeks. There was something decidedly odd in the way these figures were moving, like stiff-jointed puppets, and it was only when I got close to one of them that I realised they were scarecrows.

I almost jumped out of my skin when the head turned to look at me. Its eyes were Xs stitched in thick black twine and the mouth widened into an uncomfortable smile, revealing dried corn kernels for teeth.

"I'm sorry, I didn't mean to disturb you," I shouted over my shoulder, walking away as quickly as I could. I told myself to keep looking ahead, not to turn around to check whether the scarecrows were following me.

Finally I came to the Old Green Grumble's shed. It was easy to recognise as it was by far the most shambolic of all the buildings. In fact, I'd go as far as to say, it was the most shambolic thing I'd ever seen, anywhere. It seemed to defy physics as it leant at such an awkward angle that it appeared to be held together with nothing but a few nails and good faith. The single window was so filthy it would have been impossible to see in, let alone for him to see out and I was sure that was how he preferred it. I was now within ten steps of the shed, when suddenly the door swung open and out came the Old Green Grumble, shaking his fist, stamping from one foot to the other.

"You gerroorff, geddoutt, snotbag!" growled the old Green Grumble.

I fought the urge to run. Instead I plucked up all my courage and spoke. "Excuse me sir, sorry to trouble you, I was hoping to have a quick word."

"Why'd I wanna speak wiv an hobble lil' so an' so like you. Go on, naff off!"

I was determined to say my piece, even if it meant I would have to endure more of his shouting and the rotten cabbage-like smell that he gave off. "I have something for you," I said.

"Din wannit, blummin loada ol' rubbish probly!" Here he turned to go back to his shed, perhaps to fetch his shotgun.

I called out to him. "It's from the Pig Man, he says you needed a new lamp?"

He stopped, with his hand clutching the piece of rope serving as a door handle.

"The Pig Man has found you a lamp. He says it was in his workshop. Apparently, it works perfectly well."

The Old Green Grumble mumbled to himself, then

turned around to face me. I held out the lamp for him to see and he shuffled towards me. Quick as a flash, he grabbed the lamp from my hand, turned around and scuttled back inside the shed, slamming the door behind him.

"You rude, ungrateful old—" I was stomping towards the shed, ready to give him a piece of my mind when suddenly the door swung open again and the Old Green Grumble gingerly stepped towards me. He took out something from the pocket of his mouldy old cardigan and placed it in my hand. It was a small wooden mouse, with fishing wire whiskers and a parcel string tail. It was exquisite.

"Did you carve this yourself?" I asked.

"Might a' dun," he replied croakily, and ambled back inside the shed, gently closing the door behind him. I stood for a minute or so, staring at the little wooden mouse. Then I popped it in my pocket and walked home, smiling all the way.

CHAPTER 16

A PROMISE

Mum and I were watching TV together.

"Have you seen Hewett lately?" she asked.

"Not recently," I said, my attention fixed to the screen, where Tony Hart had started drawing on to a piece of paper.

"Margaret says you haven't called round for him in quite a while. Have you fallen out with each other?" I felt a wave of sadness pass through me. I'd spent so much time by myself lately, I'd begun to lose touch with my friends.

"Maybe, Hewett could come over for tea tomorrow?" said Mum.

"Can we have French Bread Pizzas?" I asked excitedly.

"Yes, why not," replied Mum. "I'll phone Margaret to let her know."

On the flickering screen, Tony's drawing was coming together. With broad sweeps of red and yellow chalk pastels he'd created a sunset across the top half of the paper and was now using a thick black marker to create a group of standing stones silhouetted against the sky.

"Wow I'd love to try doing that," I said,

"I bet you'd do a wonderful job of it" said Mum.

"I don't have any pastels."

"Well why don't you go to Baily and Woods tomorrow morning, I'll let you have your pocket money early. You could ask Hewett along."

"Brilliant," I said, "thanks Mum."

Baily and Woods would best be described as a mini emporium, located in the centre of town, next to the much admired parish church. The small shop seemed to be packed from floor to ceiling with everything imaginable; keyrings, fizzy drinks, sweets, books, magazines, comics, calendars, jigsaw puzzles, Airfix model kits, tiny porcelain Wade Wimsies, Matchbox cars and egg-shaped, hollow-eyed Weebles. Between the front area of the shop and the back room stood a large black oil burner, from which the smell of gasoline permeated the building. When in use, the boiler would be blazing red hot, and it was nothing short of miracle that no child had been seriously injured by coming into contact with it.

Beyond this lay the back room which was filled with neat arrangements of stationery; ring binders, notepads, exercise books, pencils, biros, bottles of fountain pen ink, boxes of elastic bands, pencil-top rubbers, books of raffle tickets, packets of stamp hinges and bottles of amber coloured glue. I would happily spend hours roaming around, deciding what to spend my pocket money on, taking in the heady blend of smells and aromas.

On this occasion, I managed to find some coloured chalks, probably not as good quality as the ones Tony Hart had been using but they still cost the best part of that week's pocket money. I pictured the image I wanted to create; of the Lonely Clown's shack and the trees in the copse, silhouetted against a lemon and violet Otherlands sky.

As we were walking home, Hewett offered me a pack of Super Bazooka bubble gum and I set about unwrapping it carefully so as not to tear the tiny comic strip inside. Even better than the comic strip was the special offer, and on this occasion it was for a pair of X-Ray goggles. I remembered what the Oak Mother had said to me and Aislinn that time, how we were able to see through the veil that separated our world from the Otherlands. I wondered if my friends could use the X-Ray goggles to look through the veil, and see what I had seen.

"What have you been drawing lately then, I haven't seen any of your stuff for ages?" said Hewett, snapping me out of my thoughts. I wanted to tell him about the drawings I'd been making of the Pig Man, the Trolls and the Oak Mother's house in the garden with the huge toadstools.

Then I remembered my promise to the Oak

Mother that I wouldn't tell any of my friends about the Otherlands. She'd told me to keep it a secret, that only children like me and Aislinn were allowed to know about it.

"Oh just some stupid cartoons, animals and things like that," I replied, before quickly changing the subject. "Anyway, my special offer is a pair of X-Ray goggles, what's yours?"

"Camping knife," replied Hewett before blowing a bubble the size of a tennis ball. The bubble popped with a sharp smacking sound and Hewett continued to read from his piece of paper while chewing loudly at the same time.

"It's got four blades, a can opener, leather hole punch and a screwdriver."

"Woah, that's cool."

"Not as cool as X-Ray goggles though. I mean, imagine being able to see through walls and stuff."

"Yeah, that's pretty cool," I replied, half smiling to myself.

CHAPTER 17

INTRUDERS

Something was stirring in the earth at the edge of the Oak Mother's garden. Stubby fingers poked through the soil, followed by hands and arms, then a head. With much spluttering and coughing, an oddly shaped figure climbed out of the ground.

There followed another figure, then two more and finally there were four of them. They stood shaking the soil from their leathery skin while they took in their surroundings. They had emerged on the slope of grassland not far from the mouth of the spell chamber. Here the group of standing stones stood around them, expressing their disapproval at this intrusion through a series of deep mumbling sounds.

"What's that horrible smell?" said one of the creatures.

"I think it's called fresh air," said another.

"It's making my eyes water," said the third.

"Keep your voices down, you idiots," said the fourth figure, who was clearly the leader.

"Sorry my Lord," said the first, "we promise we'll be

as quiet as little spores settling on a mouldy log."

"You'd better had be. Now show me the map."

Two of the figures unfolded a map and held it open, tilting it so it could be seen in the moonlight.

"Right then, according to this it's not far from here," said the leader, pointing at the map, "just at the end of this pathway."

They proceeded in the direction of the spell chamber and once they arrived, rather than brushing aside the creeper, they yanked and pulled away great handfuls of it to reveal the opening in the rock face. They shambled into the cave and there in the centre, was the plinth. The lead figure hobbled up to it and took out a flat slab of stone from the sack hanging over his shoulder.

He placed the slab on the plinth and brushed the soil from its surface to reveal some letters that had been crudely chiselled there. These sharp angular marks formed words written in Underlandish.

"Right then, shut up you lot," said Bowelcreep, "not a word, not a sound, otherwise you'll ruin it all."

He stared at the tablet for a moment, pointed to the words and then started to speak. His voice produced sounds like those made by rocks being split and of dry wood being burned. He spoke as if every word was born of bitterness and resentment, using a language as old as daylight. These words formed a dark spell, a curse, rotten as carrion and potent as venom.

Other sounds were beginning to fill the cave, the sounds of things struggling for air, of creatures crying in the dark and nightmares singing of their impending arrival.

Bowelcreep's guards were hopping from leathery foot to leathery foot, waving their knotty limbs and grinning with tombstone teeth, ecstatic in the maelstrom that hissed and crackled around them. The sound reached an ear-bleeding level before grinding down and choking itself into silence. Then there was laughter, the ugly laughter of hyenas taunting their victim.

Bowelcreep lifted the stone tablet above his head and slammed it down, shattering it into several pieces on the cave floor.

Then the four of them walked out of the cave, hacking and roaring with delight. Upon returning to the grass slope they directed verbal insults at the standing stones before scrabbling back down into the earth from whence they came. The air in the garden had already started to turn stale.

CHAPTER 18

KEEPING A SECRET

The three of us were hanging out under the railway bridge – me, Michael and Hewett – where we'd discovered an abandoned Vespa scooter lying on its side in the verge. It took all our combined strength to heave the thing out of the undergrowth and set it upright. Both wheels had been removed, so it stood fairly stable as all three of us sat on the seat.

The bike had clearly come to an untimely end – the front mudguard now veered off at an odd angle from the handlebars. There were ten or so mirrors attached to the front, so obviously it had at one time been the pride and joy of a local Mod, but now many of the mirrors were smashed or cracked, and the brackets were bent or hanging limply from their fastenings. It didn't matter to us. For a while we were jewel thieves riding a stolen Harley Davidson through the streets of San Francisco, with twenty motorcycle cops hot on our tail.

Eventually we left the scooter and climbed up to the top of the embankment. We sat down and took a moment to study the graffiti that had been sprayed on the walls beneath the bridge; *Man Utd Rule, Anarchy in the UK, Sharon is a slag.* We giggled at the crude renderings of willies and boobs while we threw stones at an empty paint tin lying on the ground below us. Now seemed like the ideal moment. I took a deep breath and began speaking.

"I've got something to tell you, but please don't think I'm mental." Hewett and Michael looked at each other and immediately started sniggering.

"Honestly, it's really important."

They looked in opposite directions, to avoid making eye contact and triggering more laughter.

"There's this place, ok, and it's full of creatures and beings from our nightmares. They start in our imagination, they're born in a burst of electrical energy. But they're trapped in a half-formed state. They get agitated and angry and start calling to us. That's when we see them. My friend Aislinn has seen them too. They can be brought to life and that's when they get sent to the Otherlands where they become fully-formed beings."

The two of them burst into hysterics.

"Look shut up will you. I need you to listen. You've seen them too. The Swan Lady—"

"Yeah, but she isn't real. We're just messing about."

"But you talked about her. I thought you'd seen them. I thought you knew!"

"It's just a story Skinners." The laughter continued, and Hewett made a few cuckoo noises, while twirling his finger in a circular motion at the side of his temple.

"Don't bother then, see if I care." I climbed over the wall and stormed off in the direction of City Bank. I felt in my pocket and there it was, the mouse given to me by the Old Green Grumble. I stroked the whiskers and twirled the tail around my finger.

"See, I'm not making it up," I whispered to the mouse and carefully put it back in my pocket. I would run without stopping, all the way to City Bank, along the top of the embankment to the gap in the trees. I would slide down the side of the embankment, not caring if the stones and brambles scratched my skin and I would slip through the opening in the veil to find myself once more in the Otherlands.

I arrived at the meadow and there was Aislinn standing in the stream, busily picking through the vegetation growing on the bank. The Oak Mother was standing over her, giving instructions.

"Now, carefully cup a clutch of leaves and tease it gently."

Aislinn was concentrating intensely as she slowly pulled the plant, roots and all from the soil. She held it up for the Oak Mother to see.

"Perfect. Now see if you can find a few more like that."

Aislinn placed the plant in a sack slung across her shoulder and moved on to the next patch.

"Hello Aislinn, do you need a hand?" Aislinn turned to look at me and sighed a deep sad sigh.

"What's wrong?" I asked, "What's happened?"

"The Swan Lady's crows heard you talking to your friends," said the Oak Mother without hesitation.

"What? They heard me? But how?"

"It's a very thin veil between our two worlds. The crows see and hear everything, including the sound of promises being broken."

"I'm so sorry. I didn't mean to blab. It's just that my friends noticed that I haven't been around as much and …"

"The others have called a meeting. They're going to decide what should be done."

"I won't be punished, will I?" I said, suddenly afraid. "They won't give me the cane or something like that, will they?"

"No, I'm sure they won't hurt you. But they may decide to banish you from the Otherlands."

"But that's not fair. I created them remember."

"This is their world, not yours," said the Oak Mother. "They have their ways and rules, and you have to respect that."

I felt so ashamed and embarrassed.

"I promise I won't say any more to my friends. They didn't believe me any way."

"It's too late, I'm afraid," said the Oak Mother. "The rules are there to protect the balance between our two worlds. When one of those rules is broken, that balance is threatened."

I stood there with the stream skipping about my feet and watched as the Oak Mother breathed in and began making a most peculiar sound, a throaty tremolo that travelled out into the trees nearby. I heard a gentle rustling coming from the one of the branches arching out over the stream. An egret was perched there, tilting its head down towards us. The Oak Mother carried on calling to it, and the egret answered back with the same croaky sounds. With a dip of its body and an unfurling of its bright white wings, the egret took off and headed out, over the meadow towards the Pig Man's house.

"The egret will be our messenger. Soon, the others will know where and when to meet. We must be on our way, we don't want to be late."

"Where are we going?"

"To meet the others," she said, "by the stone table at Monk's Mound."

CHAPTER 19

THE MEETING

It was a fair distance from the meadow to Monk's Mound. The low growl of thunder rippled across the sky and there was a metallic taste to the soft breeze whirling around us. Lightning had released nitrogen into the air, which fell to the earth in a barrage of plump raindrops. Plants drank greedily in the downpour and our surroundings became bathed in green light radiating from their leaves.

As we headed out across the fields the clouds started to break up, revealing blue sky. Sunlight rolled towards us like a silent ocean wave, and I pinched myself, realising that had this been my home-world, we would have been walking straight down the middle of the dual carriageway.

We walked out through waist-high wheat towards Monk's Mound, which stood like an island in a sea of pale gold. The group of elm trees standing on top of the mound were swaying in the breeze, welcoming us with their ritual dance. The Lonely Clown was sitting with his back against one of the trees, playing a sad Bluesy tune on his harmonica.

The Old Green Grumble was skulking on the other side of the mound, while the Pig Man kept an eye on his pigs as they wandered about, snouts snuffling in the soil. Rat Kid was sitting in the crook of a tree branch, nibbling on an ear of wheat. The trolls were absent, presumably snoozing in their cave, out of reach of the sun's rays. The Swan Lady's crows were doing their best to intimidate the white egret, who had taken prime position on a branch overhanging the stone table.

This large flat limestone slab rested on four smaller blocks, the carved markings on its surface were peppered with lichen and moss. Seats made from beechwood were set out neatly around the edge, and on one of these, sitting cross-legged, humming to herself, was The Oak Mother. The top of her head was just visible above the table.

Next to her was a large figure whose head was adorned with a tall crown made of twigs and leaves. His face was the colour of sage, framed with mossy hair and an impressive beard of ivy. He was clutching a large wooden tankard in one hand, while holding a twisted wooden staff in the other. He drank from the tankard, and let forth a thunderous belch, causing the pigs to cease their snuffling momentarily and look up.

As if on cue, the others came to find their place at the table. Once everybody was seated the Oak Mother spoke.

"Dear Otherlanders, I welcome you all to this most

sacred place and I offer thanks to his Honour, the Green Man, who graces us with his presence as overseer of this meeting."

The figure tapped his staff against the edge of the table before taking another swig from his tankard. The Oak Mother continued.

"I have called you here today to discuss what action should be taken against this child, who in a moment of carelessness has broken his promise not to reveal the existence of the Otherlands."

I dropped my head, eyes fixed to the ground as whispers and grunts of disapproval sounded from around the table.

"Chuck 'im out!" came the voice of the Old Green Grumble, and I shrank even further into my body. "Too many of 'em 'ere already, makin' nuisances of 'emselves."

"I haven't been a nuisance, I've been helping. I brought you the lamp, remember?" The Old Green Grumble muttered something under his breath and turned his back on me.

"The child has been very helpful," said the Lonely Clown.

"And he seems friendly enough," said Rat Kid.

"The fact is a promise has been broken," said the Green Man, in his rich baritone, "and there may well be consequences."

The Oak Mother was now stood up in her seat. "There is a fine balance that exists between our two worlds. As more and more humans become aware of our existence, there is danger of that balance being destroyed," she said solemnly.

"I'll tell my friends I didn't mean any of it – I'll say that none of it's true and I was just joking."

"He's broken one promise already. How do we know he's to be trusted?" came a voice from overhead. The rest of us looked up to see Creeping Jenny standing on a branch high up in the tree. She stared down at me with a look that showed she had not forgotten our previous encounter when I'd run at her screaming, trying to scare her away. I looked around in desperation.

"Trial by Bugbear," shouted the Old Green Grumble, and the others nodded in agreement, all except Rat Kid and the Lonely Clown who shook their heads.

"What's trial by Bugbear?" I asked, already dreading the answer.

"Surely, we don't need to go that far?" shouted Rat Kid.

"Bugbear, Bugbear, Bugbear!" chanted the others. Aislinn looked at me and saw the terrified look on my face.

"Don't you think he deserves a second chance?" she said to the others.

"We can't go making exceptions," said the Swan Lady.

"Not even for your creator?" said Aislinn and a hush fell immediately on the congregation. I shifted uncomfortably as I watched the others form a huddle around the Oak Mother. After a few minutes of intense muttering and shushing the others went back to their seats, leaving the Swan Lady to speak on their behalf.

"He may be a creator but if we are to live in harmony we must all abide by the same rules." she said and the others began nodding their heads again.

The Green Man stood with his arms folded across his chest. "All those who agree that the boy should face trial by Bugbear, please raise your hands." Everyone put their hands above their heads except for the Clown and Rat Kid, who sat with their heads bowed. The Green Man drank the last of his ale and banged the empty tankard back down on the table.

"The decision has been made. The child will face trial by Bugbear." There was more animated chattering from the others as the Green Man walked around the table to where I was standing.

"Come with me child, the Bugbear's cave is not far from here," he said, and he led me away from the table.

"Can I come too?" said Aislinn running after us, "I think Steven should have someone to keep him company."

I looked to the Green Man, my heart pounding. The Green Man thought for a moment.

"Very well," he replied. "I respect your show of friendship and bravery young Aislinn. You may come with us."

I felt an immense wave of gratitude as the three of us walked across the field, carefully passing through the tall stalks of wheat. I finally plucked up the courage to ask what had been playing on my mind.

"What exactly is the Bugbear?" I whispered to Aislinn with a tremble in my voice.

"I think at some point, he was a man," she whispered back.

The Green Man overheard us. "That's right and a whole lot of trouble he was too, always up to no good."

"What sort of things did he do?" I asked

"Stealing, trespassing, being drunk and disorderly and no matter how many times he got caught, he couldn't stop himself. Got to the point if clothes went missing from a washing line, a window got broken or a barn caught fire, you could be sure he was responsible. Eventually, the local folk decided they'd had enough. They appointed a sorcerer to cast a spell, transforming that wretch into the cantankerous creature we now know as the Bugbear. From then on, he's roamed the woods and countryside, scaring off children who might be getting up to mischief."

"So they don't turn out like he did?" suggested Aislinn.

"That's right," said the Green Man. "The Bugbear will be the one to decide if you are to be trusted or not, young lad."

"How will he decide?" I asked, struggling to keep up.

"He has his ways," said the Green Man, pressing on towards the edge of the woods.

CHAPTER 20

THE BUGBEAR

Even though Aislinn and The Green Man were walking either side of me, I felt the comfort of their presence dwindling as we drew nearer to the woods. The inky clouds had returned to the sky and the sun struggled to cast its watery light. The Swan Lady's crows were cawing noisily overhead, seeming to mock me as they followed us to the edge of the field. We came to a gap in the wall that marked the entrance to the woods and sitting there was a curious figure dressed in a cream coloured smock and floppy wide-brimmed hat.

"Hello Amaethon, thank you for allowing us to cross your field," said the Green Man. The figure jumped down from the wall and stood to attention.

"My pleasure, your grace." He took off his hat to reveal dark brown hair that fell in thick curls about his rosy face. Then he pointed at me. "That the young one causing all the trouble then?"

"You'd know all about causing trouble wouldn't you, Amaethon," said the Green Man, giving him a wink and a wry smile.

"Ah, you're right there," said Amaethon, letting forth a mischievous chuckle. "Careful how you go," he said, pointing at the opening to the woods, "Bugbear's been grumbling and groaning all morning. Reckon it knows you're coming." He looked at me and grinned, before bowing and ushering us past with a flamboyant wave of his arm.

"Take no notice of him, he can't help himself," said the Green Man as we entered the woods.

"Who is he?" I asked.

"Believe it or not, he was once a Lord."

"Really? He looks like one of the Wurzels."

"He was born in the land of the red dragon, among the mountains and valleys of the beautiful Otherland of Annwn. Goodness knows what possessed him, but one day he stole three animals that belonged to King Arawn and as punishment he was rejected by his family and banished. After many a day's wandering, he arrived in this Otherland and he's been here ever since. He spends his days turning the soil and tending to the crops. That is, of course, when he isn't lazing about or making a nuisance of himself."

The light was starting to dim as we approached the area of pine trees at the northwest point of the woods. I scanned between the tall straight trunks, looking for any sign of the Bugbear. We came to where the ground sloped downwards into a deep pit, the walls of which were covered in bracken and ivy. The Green Man used his thick legs and wide feet to make a track through the undergrowth and we followed him for twenty yards or so to a part of the wall where a dark patch appeared behind the foliage.

"This must be the door to the Bugbear's den," said Aislinn. "Let's hope he's not asleep."

"Bogil, are you there?" shouted the Green Man, loud enough to wake the dead let alone a sleeping Bugbear.

"Only if you intend not to waste my time," came a low growl from inside the cave, and the Green Man made his way through the curtain of ivy, leading me by the hand with Aislinn following us.

My eyes adjusted to the darkness as we moved through a short passageway. We came to a chamber that had been hollowed out of the earth. A fire crackled and spat from a recess set in one of the walls and by its light we could make out a large figure sitting on a chair built from gnarled oak branches.

His arms were as thick as my waist, and covered in coarse brown hair, or fur. His hands were resting on his lap, fingers stretched out to reveal long black fingernails. His face was hidden beneath the hood of his coat, but I could make out the stubby muzzle from which protruded curved yellow tusks.

"Bogil, we thank you for allowing us into your home," said the Green Man.

"I don't suppose I can object," rumbled the Bugbear begrudgingly.

"This child has broken a promise. He has revealed the existence of the Otherlands to two of his human friends. We believe he was not acting maliciously, more that his emotions got the better of him."

"Emotions have much to answer for," grunted the Bugbear.

"He is my friend, and he meant no harm," said Aislinn.

"Whether he meant harm or not, actions have consequences. Bring him forward," said the Bugbear. I froze, my body rigid with fear. The Green Man leant forward and whispered in my ear.

"He will not hurt you, trust me."

Reluctantly, quaking, I took a few steps and stood in front of the Bugbear. I closed my eyes and shuddered as I felt his hands being placed on top of my head. I kept my eyes closed, and I could hear his breathing become deep and slow. My mind began to swirl with images, the river by the Pig Man's house teeming with litter; pop cans and carrier bags. The opening to the troll's cave, closed by a brick wall, and criss-crossed with barbed wire. I saw cages, shadowy figures hunched inside, then the Swan Lady was reaching her arm out to me through the bars.

Next I was looking down at my bedroom, as if I were floating near the ceiling. I saw three or four ugly grey-skinned creatures throwing my books about the room and breaking my toys, while a large black dog was tearing my bedsheets with its teeth and claws. It turned its head upwards and fixed me with eyes the colour of blood.

I screamed and opened my eyes, and saw the Bugbear on his chair in front of me, his arms now crossed over his chest, his head bowed.

"It is done," he said. Aislinn and the Green Man took this as their cue to lead me out of the cave. Once outside, I sat against the wall of the pit, my eyes stinging in the daylight.

"Was that the future?" I asked.

"No, merely a vision of what might be," replied the Green Man.

"I'm sorry! I've been so stupid."

"Child, you are not stupid. You are still learning," said the Green Man. "We're all still learning. It never stops."

We made our way back through the trees, eager to reach the open space of the wheat field before the onset of the gloaming.

CHAPTER 21

NAN AND BAMP

The next day, I went with dad to visit Nan and Bamp and as usual Bamp was pottering about in his vegetable garden at the back of the house. He was always busy, whether it was picking gooseberries for Nan to make into jam or pulling up the onions ready for pickling. He looked up from his work as we arrived and gave us both a smile.

"Here's young Crack-at-it," he said fondly, before getting back to work. This was the nickname he'd given to me at the age of six, when I was offered prawn cocktail at a family meal in Leo's Italian restaurant. I'd never heard of prawn cocktail before, and I was slightly wary as to what I might be letting myself in for.

"Go on then," I'd said after a short deliberation, "I'll have a crack at it."

Bamp had never forgotten it.

Dad and I walked in through the back door, into the kitchen and there was Nan, busy cooking lunch. Dad sat down at the small foldaway table and started reading the newspaper while Nan chatted to him about the cricket. I made my way through the hallway into the living room and there it was again, that familiar smell of furniture polish. There was also the slight ammonia tang of Brasso which Bamp used to polish his skittles trophies, something he did religiously every Sunday morning. They were arranged along the shelf that ran around two sides of the living room, and they sparkled in the sunlight that came pouring through the windows.

I sat down in Nan's high-backed chair and heard the seat springs creak as they took my weight. The radio next to me was playing Radio 4's Sunday Service, which this week was coming from King's College, Cambridge. The choir were singing *Panis Angelicus*. I closed my eyes and the sound of the music hung in the air like nebula suspended in the vastness of space. I felt my body sink deeper into the chair as those voices swam about my head in swathes of amber coloured light.

I'm not sure how long I was asleep for, but I was woken by Dad, telling me it was time to go home. I realised how very tired I had become these last few days, and it seemed the extra work, the writing, the drawing and all that sneaking back and forth, as well as the excitement and apprehension, had started to catch up with me. I sleepily stumbled into the kitchen where Nan was making gravy and I waved goodbye as I headed out the door.

"Goodness me, you must be tired young man," said Nan "you haven't asked to choose your sweets."

"Oh crikey!" I said, suddenly springing back to life, "Please Nan, may I choose my sweets?"

"Of course you can my dear," said Nan bringing the enormous sweet jar out from the tiny walk-in larder. "You'd better choose some for your brother too, otherwise you know what will happen."

"Yes, thank you Nan."

"We can't have you two falling out over a few sweets, can we now," said Nan.

"Heaven forbid," sighed Dad, and waited as I carefully picked out six sweets for me and six sweets for my brother. I made sure to include a couple of banana flavour Toffos as these were his favourite. We said goodbye to Nan and walked out of the house, back into the garden, where Bamp was pottering about inside his greenhouse.

"Cheerio then, Crack-at-it," he said as he began watering the tomatoes.

"Bye Bamp," I said, popping a pear drop into my mouth.

"I'll see you up at the cricket later then," said Dad.

"Only if I can fix the puncture on my bike, else I'll not bother. What about you Crack-at-it, you going too?"

"Not likely, cricket's boring."

"He'll be up in his room, doing his drawings," said Dad.

"You'll have to bring some round next time, let your nan and me see what you've been up to lately."

I thought of the drawings I'd been working on that morning, of Creeping Jenny hiding behind the talking stones, waiting to pounce on a couple of unsuspecting kids. "Alright, but you might think they're a bit weird."

"I wouldn't expect anything less, young man," he said, and smiled as he waved us goodbye.

CHAPTER 22

THE WANING CURSE

It was early Monday morning and I had just stepped out into the Oak Mother's garden. I looked around me, sensing things were somehow not quite right. Was it my imagination or had the sky turned a sort of dull paper towel grey? The leaves on the trees, weren't they now a sludgy boiled cabbage green? The flowers; had they not lost their luminance? In fact, had they not started closing their petals? I looked up at the sun and, rather than having to squint as I normally would on a summer morning, I could look straight into its centre, my eyes wide open. It looked almost semi-transparent, like a communion wafer being help up to a candle.

In a confused daze I walked into the cave, where I hoped to find the Oak Mother, and sure enough there she was and Aislinn too. They were standing amidst books and scrolls that had been roughly scattered about the floor. There was a stack of books, piled haphazardly on the plinth, and the Oak Mother was frantically flicking through the pages of one. Aislinn ran over to me.

"Is everything ok?" I asked, sensing the air of panic.

"No dear child, far from it," said the Oak Mother

"Something's wrong isn't it, something outside?" I said.

"The Waning, you mean?" She continued to turn the pages rapidly.

"The what, sorry?" I asked

"The Waning. Our daylight is disappearing."

"I *thought* something had changed. It feels like it's the evening. What's going on?"

She continued leafing vigorously through the book, seemingly oblivious to my question. The awful thought crossed my mind that this was my fault, that this was part of the vision Bugbear had given. Aislinn seemed lost for words as she stood next to me, biting her fingernails.

Out of sheer desperation I shouted, "Please Oak Mother, what is happening, you're frightening me now, please tell me!"

"I am so sorry child, I do indeed owe you an explanation. Oh how foolish I have been." She took a moment's pause. "There is a place that exists, below us, deep beneath the earth. This place is called The Underlands. The beings that live here are called Underlanders; mean twisted creatures that skulk about in their dark caverns and chambers underground."

She gave a shudder. "Then there's Bowelcreep."

"What's Bowelcreep?"

"Bowelcreep is ruler of the Underlands. Not through

fair and reasonable means mind you, he's just connived his way into power and bullied many of the others into becoming his soldiers. Now it would seem, he has set a waning curse upon our lands."

"Why would he do that, why would he be so cruel?" I asked.

"His cruelty is born of deep resentment. He has always despised us. He feels that those who live in the Underlands have been punished by Nature itself, condemned to live in darkness, discarded, shut out of sight. Through the years their anger has been allowed to fester, passed through blood and set into their bones. Bowelcreep has devoted most of his life to stoking this anger, turning us into their enemy. I believe he's planning to take over the Otherlands."

"So what are we going to do?" I asked.

"The Oak Mother's been searching for a way to break the curse, but this is Dark Magic," said Aislinn, "Apparently, the only being that can reverse it is the being that cast it. Bowelcreep himself."

"How on earth are we going to persuade him to reverse the curse?"

"Not through gentle persuasion, that's for sure," answered the Oak Mother.

"Shouldn't we tell the others what's happened?" said Aislinn. "They will already have noticed that something is drastically wrong."

"Yes child, it's only right that they should know."

"Who shall we visit first?"

"We don't have time to visit them individually. I will have to summon them here."

She began lifting the books off of the plinth and placing them carefully on the floor. Next she walked over to one of the recesses in the wall, lifted out the crystal that had been set there and carried it to the plinth. She pulled a small powder blue velvet book from the pile at her feet, turned a few pages until she found the right one and placed a hand on the crystal. She whispered the words written on the open page and the crystal began to emit a warm glow the colour of tropical seas. As the glow intensified, I watched a thin beam of light shoot up from the crystal towards the ceiling of the cave. The tips of the roots poking through the rock began to glow the same colour as the crystal. The ceiling was now twinkling like the night sky.

"Now you two, come with me." The Oak Mother walked out of the chamber, as quickly as her short legs would carry her. We followed her outside.

"Look up there!" she said pointing to the tree that grew on top of the cave. The leaves were glowing the same turquoise colour. The light radiated out and filled the air around it.

"Now they'll know where to come," said the Oak Mother. We sat down on the grass in front of the cave, and waited.

CHAPTER 23

ROCKS AND MOULDY THINGS

"When do we get to go back up top, my Lord?" asked Mulch, in his most polite tone.

"When it's dark enough, idiot!" groaned Bowelcreep.

"And how long will that be, do you think, my Lord?"

"How would I know. Look I've cast the spell and according to our scouts, it's working. So for now, stop asking stupid questions." There was a short silence before Swallet piped up.

"I can't wait to finally walk around in all that open space, with no rotten sunlight to burn our skin."

"Or blind our eyeballs," added Gryke.

"Yeah, and no more squatting down here all hunched up, damp and miserable," said Dante.

"Yeah, I'm sick of staring at rocks and mouldy things, and them drips that come down through the roof, drip, drip, drip, drip, drip," said Ruckle before Bowelcreep raised his knobbly arm above his knobbly head.

He waited for silence. "It will be our finest hour. Once we've taken over the Otherlands, the whole of the

Toplands will be ours to do with whatever we want."

There was much cheering and shouting, which sounded like someone gargling broken glass while mistreating an animal.

CHAPTER 24

THE SUN STAR

Soon a small crowd had gathered in front of the cave. The Swan Lady and the Lonely Clown were there already, talking with Aislinn and the Oak Mother. Rat Kid stood leaning against the wall of the cave, licking her hand and using it to wash the backs of her ears. The Pig Man was standing some distance from the others and the Old Green Grumble was there also, hidden in a clump of ferns set to one side of the cave entrance, grumbling to itself. Last of all, came the Trolls, clearly struggling with being awake at this time of day. At least the light was dim enough that they could survive being outside at this early hour. The Oak Mother cleared her throat. Once she had everyone's attention, she stepped into the centre of our throng and acknowledged each member in turn with a bow of her head. After a moment's silence, she spoke to us.

"My dear friends, good beings of the Otherlands. I have called you here as a matter of urgency." I could hear a nervous flutter in the Oak Mother's voice. "We are in great danger. Bowelcreep has cast a waning curse upon our land. Daylight is fading fast. There will be the most disastrous consequences."

"My pigs won't eat," said the Pig Man.

"My birds won't go in their pond," said the Swan Lady, "the water's all murky."

"Scarecrows tell me the vegetables are turning bad," grumbled the Old Green Grumble.

"And we can't get any sleep," said one of the trolls.

"I hear you my friends and believe me this is just the beginning. It will get a lot worse."

"What can we do?" asked Aislinn.

"The only way we can break the curse is to persuade Bowelcreep himself to break it," said the Oak Mother.

"A's never gon'appen," grumbled the Old Green Grumble.

"I truly believe anything is possible, as long as we put our minds together." The Oak Mother's eyes were twinkling with tears.

"Follow our hearts and work as one!" added Rat Kid enthusiastically.

"The only way to defeat Dark Magic, is with light. That light must come from the purest source."

She took from her pocket a small glass bottle and held it out in front of her. Inside the bottle was a tiny white flower. *"This* is that source. This is the Sun Star. It is said to have been blessed in the light of the first dawn."

We stared at the little flower, mesmerised.

"Over the years the Sun Star has been protected by

many spells to help preserve it, but now as the daylight fades, so too the Sun Star's power fades. We have very little time. We must travel together into the Underlands. We must find Bowelcreep so that I can force him to reverse his spell."

"Best o' luck," said the Old Green Grumble sarcastically.

"Well yes, a little bit of luck is always useful," said the Oak Mother, "But we can't leave it all to chance and luckily, I have a plan …"

Aislinn and I began scurrying about finding cloth bags and filling them with berries, biscuits and pouches of water and before long everyone was equipped with their own bag of provisions.

There was a clamour of conversation as we assembled into some sort of pack. Led by the Oak Mother, we proceeded through the garden and out along the embankment.

In a short time we came to a place where a tree grew out of the side of the embankment. Its trunk was curved like a question mark, the branches reaching down as if to claw at the ground beneath it. The Oak Mother walked to the base of the tree, where some roots were poking through the earth. She took out a small phial from her pocket, uncorked it and sprinkled the contents on to the roots. Almost instantly, the roots began moving to reveal an opening in the earth.

"Here it is. The way in," said the Oak Mother. A gust of cold damp air passed through us, and the rich smell of dark earth filled our noses. The Oak Mother turned to face the sky and raised her walking cane above her head, chanting quietly.

"What's she doing?" I whispered to the Swan Lady.

"She's casting out a blessing spell across our lands. It's like leaving a note to say we'll be gone for some time, but we'll be back."

"And will we be back?" I asked.

"We must stay hopeful," she replied, offering only the slightest of smiles. Once the Oak Mother's spell had been completed, we gathered ourselves and headed into the Underlands.

CHAPTER 25

THE UNDERLANDS

On the edge of a subterranean lake, the armies of the Underlands were busy making preparations. Some were cutting tree roots into thin strips, ready to wind them together to make lengths of rope. This rope would be used to bind their captives.

Others were chiselling lumps of flint into sharp axe heads and strapping them to handles made from thicker pieces of root. These axes would be used to cut down the trees of Otherland and they would use the wood to make cages for their captives.

There was a purposefulness about the Underlanders rarely seen before. It seemed the prospect of conflict and devastation was a great incentive to them.

We were making our way through the vast network of tunnels, passages, crawlspaces and caves that made up the Underlands. Lit by the Sun Star, our progress at times was laboured due to the unforgiving terrain. Occasionally, steps had been carved out of the steepest rock faces, and chasms had been spanned by bridges made from root rope.

Sometimes the route became blocked by fallen rocks or landslides of earth and we would have to use our bare hands to clear the way. Other times we would stumble across a place where the light from minerals winked at us from the walls, or we'd find ourselves in a room where stalactites and stalagmites formed the jaws of a giant Underland dragon.

After a while, we came to a place where the path skirted along one side of a vast cavern. To our right, the wall stretched up to the ceiling where roots hung down way above our heads. To our left there was nothing, just a sudden vertical drop. Aislinn and I stood for a moment, looking over the edge. It felt as if we were floating over a hole that opened out into the emptiness of deep space.

Suddenly Aislinn seemed to lose her balance and she toppled against the cave wall. I grabbed her arm to prevent her falling to the floor.

"What happened, are you alright?" I asked, helping her to sit down.

"I just felt very giddy," she said.

"Do you need to rest?"

"No, I'll be fine," she replied, "as long I don't look over the edge again."

There came a loud crashing sound from further ahead as clumps of soil and small pieces of rock rained down from the ceiling on to the path. Then silence.

"What was that?" I said, as we watched a thin cloud of dust settle in front of us. It was then that something reached down from the ceiling, a limb of some sort, maybe a tree branch, gnarled and creaking. But it was flexing, like an arm or a leg.

Then there followed another and another, before a lumpen mass appeared, with six jagged limbs attached. It was a giant insect of some sort, slender legs carrying a body the size of a rhinoceros, its leathery exoskeleton covered in thick spikes.

Its triangular head twitched from side to side, searching. The vermillion coloured eyes moved in all directions. A ferocious set of mandibles opened and closed like the jaws of a piece of machinery designed to mangle metal.

Its eyes focused on a single point.

Us.

It started moving towards us.

"It's a rock mantis," yelled the Oak Mother, beginning to push the Rat Kid backwards.

"Quick, we have to turn back!" shouted the Swan Lady.

"We don't have time, we must go forward!" said the Oak Mother.

"How are we going to get past that thing, it's as wide as the path?" cried the Swan Lady.

"We have to distract it," said the Clown, and with that he picked up three decent sized rocks and started juggling with them.

He moved closer and closer to the creature until he was standing a few feet in front of it. The rock mantis's eyes were rolling in a steady circular motion, following the rocks as they spun repeatedly from the clown's hands, up and over his head and back again. The rock mantis was fixed to the spot, clearly mesmerised.

"Go on then you lot, run for it!" shouted the clown, and the rest of us dived between the front pairs of legs and crawled along the ground, the underside of the insect's body passing just above our heads.

We clambered to our feet and ran until we came to a point where the path disappeared into an opening in the wall. One by one we squeezed through the narrow gap until we were squashed together in what looked to be the start of a long tunnel. I managed to peep out through the opening to see the clown still commanding the rock mantis's attention, throwing the rocks even higher, the creature's eyes turning even wider circles.

Just then, the clown hurled the rocks over the edge of the path and the rock mantis scrabbled down the side of the chasm, chasing after them until it disappeared into the darkness below. I dived through the opening after the others. We sat, crouching on the floor, the roof barely a foot above our heads, waiting. We jumped when the clown appeared through the opening.

"Well done Corky," said the Oak Mother, "you saved our skins back there." And we gave the clown a very quiet round of applause.

The clown started to smile, before his expression

turned to one of great surprise as he started sliding backwards. We looked on in horror as two spiny front legs clasped the tails of his overcoat and began to drag him back towards the mouth of the tunnel.

Instinctively I grabbed his hand and pulled with all my strength.

"Help me, it's got him. Grab his other hand!" I yelled and Aislinn reached for the clown's outstretched arm, but she missed as the rock mantis pulled the clown away from us.

I pushed my feet against a rock to give myself extra leverage, my arms stretched to their limit, the clown groaning in agony, feeling as if his arm was about to come out of its socket. The clown's coat had become entangled in the barbed edges of the rock mantis's arms. He kicked frantically trying to break free, but he was well and truly snagged. I wasn't going to be able to hold him. Aislinn threw out her hand once more and this time she connected with the clown. Then the Pig Man reached past me and took hold as well. Together we heaved and heaved until we heard a ripping sound as the barbs tore through the fabric of the coat. In that split moment of release, we were able to drag the clown away from the insect's flailing arms. It frantically clawed at the ground, trying to reach further into the tunnel, but the opening was too narrow for it to move any closer.

Finally, the rock mantis gave up and slowly withdrew its arms from the tunnel. As a parting shot, it poked its head in through the opening and the red eyes fixed us with a piercing glare. After a few seconds the creature backed away and disappeared from view. We had hardly time to catch our breath before the Oak Mother urged us all to move on.

We crawled for what seemed like hours, struggling to breathe in the confined space, the skin on our hands and knees covered in cuts and grazes from contact with the hard rock. Finally the tunnel started to widen and the ceiling opened up, and with loud sighs of relief we arrived in a passageway tall enough that we could stand up. I stretched my legs and straightened my stiff back. Around me, the others were taking the opportunity to rest, and we ate and drank a little of our provisions. The Oak Mother passed round a pouch containing a dark green paste.

"Rub a bit of this onto any cuts and grazes," she said, "it'll help soothe the pain."

We busied ourselves tending to our injuries.

"Our next problem is this," said the Oak Mother, "The light of the Sun Star has faded so much I am struggling to see ahead of us clearly. I think the Trolls should lead now, their eyesight is more suited to these conditions."

The rest of us got to our feet and formed a line behind the trolls.

"Rat Kid, you can travel at the back, you're used to

the darkness too," added the Oak Mother. We organised ourselves into some sort of order and the trolls led us on through the passageway.

In the darkness it was impossible to spot any of the rocks and sharp stones scattered about the floor. The trolls weren't affected as the thick skin on the underside of their huge feet provided them with ample protection. They plodded on regardless while the rest of us stubbed our toes and bashed our shins as we stumbled along behind them.

"Oh dear me, this won't do," said the Oak Mother, clearly frustrated. "We must try something different." She took a small pouch from her belt, and began shaking it, making a jingling sound that echoed along the corridor. Finally, we noticed a group of pale blue lights moving towards us from the path ahead. As they came nearer, we could make out the forms of five impish beings, each glowing the colour of cornflowers.

"Hello there, Blue Caps. Thank you for responding to my call. We would very much appreciate your lighting our way. You will of course be financially rewarded."

She opened the pouch and took out a handful of coins, which she gave to the Blue Cap standing nearest to her. The Blue Caps huddled together and the coins were distributed amongst them. After a fair bit of squabbling it seemed they had reached an amicable settlement, and started walking off through the tunnel, three in front, and two at the back behind Rat Kid.

With the clear blue light emanating from our newly

acquired guides, we were able to pick up the pace, making up for lost time. It was also a huge relief to be able to see the ground beneath our feet. The Blue Caps seemed to know where we were heading, and we pressed on, ignoring the tiredness that started to seep into our muscles.

CHAPTER 26

PRISONERS

"Someone's coming" said Rat Kid urgently, her ears twitching frantically. "It sounds like Underlanders, I can hear their voices, we need to hide. Quickly."

The Blue Caps scattered themselves about the tunnel, hiding in whichever small nook or cranny they could find. The tallest troll spotted a ledge along the top of a wall of rock and set about lifting each of us up there. Between us we managed to pull up the trolls and there was just enough space for us all to fit between the ledge and the roof, so we lay there as flat and still as possible. We didn't dare to look over the edge for fear of being spotted, but we could hear their voices as they passed below us. By my guess there were at least four of them, and it sounded as if they were laughing. We waited until their voices had disappeared before cautiously clambering back down the rock face.

"Those horrible creatures were talking about our homeland," said the Oak Mother. "They said it's dark enough up there now to launch their attack. They're on their way to tell Bowelcreep."

"Let's go, we must catch up with them!" I said and we set off, following the sound of their voices, keeping a safe distance.

Before long we arrived at the end of the passageway, where a large gate was set into a wall of solid rock. The gate had been made from knotted roots and thorns crudely woven together. Clay had been packed into the mesh and sharp stones could be seen sticking out of it.

"Clearly they don't want us to get through to whatever lies on the other side," said Aislinn grimly.

"Must be where ol' Bowelcreep keeps himself hidden away," added the Swan Lady.

"We'll ne'er get that thing open," grumbled the Old Green Grumble.

"What about using one of your spells?" said the Pig Man.

"This gate's locked with more of his Dark Magic. My spells won't work," said the Oak Mother.

"Not even with the Sun Star?" I asked.

"I need to conserve its energy, I'm afraid."

"I could gnaw through those roots," said Rat Kid.

"Yes, but how long will it take? We haven't got time," said Aislinn.

"Let's just bash it down," said the big troll, and prepared to run head first at the gate.

"Wait!" hissed Aislinn, and we saw that the gate had already started to open.

We sprinted to a wide fissure in the rock and hid

there as the gate opened fully and out came groups of Underlanders pulling carts loaded with cages, axes, coils of rope and sacks filled with goodness knows what. A raiding party. There was still no sign of Bowelcreep.

We held our breath until the last of the carts had tottered along the passageway and disappeared from view. The gates had already started closing and we only just managed to slip through before they slammed shut. We found ourselves in some sort of antechamber, on the far side of which was a door. We stood listening to the sounds coming from the other side.

"Sounds like a celebration," said the Pig Man. "Noisy things, celebrations."

"They're chanting his name," said the Oak Mother. "They're chanting Bowelcreep's name."

"He must be in there," I said. "Come on, let's get him!" There were cheers from the rest of the group and we charged at the door.

"Quiet my friends," whispered the Oak Mother, barring our path. "We must stay calm. We must try to reason with them."

"I say we fight," said the Swan Lady and the rest of us sounded our agreement. Aislinn held up her hands.

"Please listen to me," Aislinn said. "The Underlanders are heavily armed and there will be many more of them than there are of us. Remember the Oak Mother's plan? We have to trust her."

There was much sighing and mumbling as we prepared to find what awaited us on the other side of the door.

"What are you doing here strangers?" came a gruff voice from behind us.

We turned round to see a large group of shaggy-haired figures, dressed in tattered furs standing not ten feet away. Some were holding up heavy axes while others were lowering lethal looking spears.

"Troglodytes," hissed the Oak Mother as the figures closed in, pointing their weapons to pin us against the wall. "Cave dwellers."

"We are here to seek council with Bowelcreep. We will not trouble you."

"And what would you possibly want from Bowelcreep?" asked the lead troglodyte.

"That is our business," replied the Oak Mother.

"Very well," said the leader, "you give us no choice." He nodded to the others and they began thrusting their spears towards us, forcing us away from the wall. Several of us tried to resist and for a moment, I wondered if we might be able to tackle them but a few quick jabs from those sharp blades soon had us moving out of the chamber.

"Where are you taking us?" demanded the Oak Mother.

"Somewhere you can't cause trouble," replied the leader.

"And what do you plan to do with us?" asked Aislinn anxiously.

"That's for our master to decide. Maybe we'll hand

you over to Bowelcreep. For a pretty price of course. Or maybe we'll keep you as our slaves."

We were taken through a series of passages that seemed to become progressively narrower and shallower. The sounds of the celebration faded away completely before we eventually arrived at the top of a steep stairway cut into the rock face. We progressed down the steps in single file. There was now total silence, which was as suffocating as the lack of air.

The dim light from the Sun Star was of little relief, merely revealing our surroundings to be nothing more than solid rock. We descended deeper and deeper. I tried desperately to banish any thoughts of my parents and my brother, of my friends and my home and my two cats, anything that might cause me to become panic stricken or despondent. It was impossible. My body trembled with wave after wave of grief and fear and my eyes were stinging. I felt Aislinn take my hand, and gently squeeze it. I saw the look of fear on her face and realised I was not alone.

Eventually we came to an iron gate, set into the rock. I heard the jangle of keys and a heavy clunking sound as the lock turned. The gate swung open and we were bustled through by the guards. The trolls resisted, standing their ground and raising their fists in a show of aggression. The troglodytes thrust their flint spear tips towards them repeatedly until the trolls gave up and followed us through the gate. We found ourselves in a small cell, no bigger than my bedroom at home.

The gate slammed shut behind us with an almighty clanging sound that almost shook the teeth from my gums.

For a while we stood motionless, not knowing what to say or what to do. One of the trolls moved over to the gate and began hammering on the rails with its huge fists. As this proved futile, it started slamming into the bars with its shoulder, again to no avail. The troll admitted defeat, and stood with its face pressed hard against the metal bars.

Tiredness struck, and it was all I could do to slump down onto the ground. As I did so, I heard a brittle crunching sound from beneath me and with horror I realised the floor was littered with bones. I leapt to my feet and shuffled backwards into a corner of the cell. I felt something poking into my back and I span round to see a gaping jaw and the eyeless sockets of a skull glaring back at me.

The skeleton's arms were outstretched, its thin wrists sitting in the metal cuffs attached to the wall by chains. I staggered backwards, more bones snapping and cracking under my feet. I stood still and that's when the sobs came over me like an unstoppable force of nature. The others huddled around me, sharing their own fears in frightened whispers. I dropped to my knees, my head sinking into my chest.

"I want to go home," I said, feeling my heart crack in two. One by one, the others sat down near me and for what seemed like an age, there was total silence.

Then, the Pig Man spoke. "Oak Mother, d'you think if you called the little blue folk they'd come and find us all the way down here?"

"If there's payment involved, they'll find us alright," she said, and began rattling her bag of coins.

After a time, we noticed a soft blue glow coming form the other side of the gate and five Blue Caps came climbing through the bars. They presented themselves to the Oak Mother and she handed out another batch of coins. As the Blue Caps bickered once more, I took the opportunity to look around me. In the half light I could see the piles of bones more clearly. There were two other skeletons, one of which was lying curled up on the ground like a child, the other sat with its back against the wall, its skull sitting atop the collar bone at a skewed angle with the few teeth that remained in place forming a gruesome grin. I quickly averted my gaze, and it was then that I noticed the Old Green Grumble bending down and picking up pieces of bone from the floor. I watched as he held up each specimen to inspect it closely. Some he discarded, throwing them to the floor. Others he placed carefully in his pocket.

Eventually, he moved over to the gate and the rest of us watched transfixed as he poked one of the bones into the lock. After some gentle pushing and turning of the bone, he tutted, removed it from the lock and threw it back down on the ground. He took another bone from his pocket and tried inserting and turning that one in the lock.

After having tried and discarded another ten or so bones, he took one more from his pocket. This one looked to be half the jawbone of an animal, perhaps a badger or a fox. A single back molar was attached to the bone and this end he inserted into the lock. He paused before giving the bone a gentle turn. There was a clicking sound. He took the bone out of the lock and placed it back in his pocket. He calmly pushed at the gate, and with a long drawn out squeak, the gate swung open.

CHAPTER 27

BACK TO THE BANQUET

With new-found energy, we made our way back up the stone stairway. We went carefully, in case someone was on guard duty, but the light from the Blue Caps made it easier to be sure.

In no time at all, we were back in the antechamber, standing at the door where we had been not two hours ago.

"This looks familiar," said Rat Kid sarcastically causing us all to chuckle quietly at the absurdity of the situation.

We could hear the noise coming from the other side of the door and realised that the Underlanders were still celebrating. Clearly, they were relishing the prospect of their upcoming triumph, and invigorated by the prospect of defeating us and destroying the Otherlands. My shoulders dropped as my heart sank.

I thought of mum, dancing around the kitchen, singing 'Tell me why, I don't like Mondays' at the top of her voice. I thought of dad watching the cricket in Bathurst Park. He'd be sitting in his deckchair, swifts and swallows darting through the air above him, a butter coloured sun beaming down.

I thought of my brother, out with his mates, kicking a football around on the school playing field, Harrington jackets and an orange swim kit bag used as goalposts.

I thought of Hewett and Michael sitting on the swings in the Golden Farm beer garden, sipping from their bottles of Cresta, enjoying each hit of strawberry fizz. I thought of my bedroom, my books and my Star Wars toys.

Desperation and delirium had taken hold.

"I could run back to my world and go to the police station," I suggested, "and tell them what's going on. They'd sort out Bowelcreep and his cronies. The police could set their alsatians on them."

"Remember what the Bugbear showed you, what would happen if our two worlds spilled into each other?" said the Oak Mother.

'What are we going to do then?" said Aislinn, anxiety creeping into her voice.

"Just let me get face to face with that vile creature," said the Oak Mother.

"Yes, but how are we going to do that?" said Rat Kid, "Listen to them, they're hungry for war, they want nothing more than to annihilate us. You think we can just walk in there unannounced and politely ask Bowelcreep to change his mind?"

"I think I might have an idea," I said in a moment of

clarity. "What if we pretend to be captured?"

Even Aislinn was staring at me in disbelief. Then a slow smile began to dawn on her mouth.

"Listen," I said. "The trolls look quite similar to the Underlanders, it's just their skin colour that is different." I turned to address the trolls directly. "You have to act as members of their army, lead us in there, and present us to Bowelcreep as your captives." The trolls looked at each other briefly, before nodding their heads in agreement.

"How are we going to disguise the trolls?" asked the Swan Lady.

"We'll use earth," I said. "We'll cover their skin with earth."

We set about scraping up handfuls of earth and clay which we then smeared over the trolls' pale green skin. It didn't take long for their faces and bodies to take on the brownish grey colour of the Underlanders. We stood back to admire our handiwork.

"Perfect." said Aislinn. "You look just like Underlanders." The trolls looked each other up and down, giggling in a way that only trolls can giggle. The Oak Mother gathered the rest of us into a huddle.

"Once we're inside," she whispered, "just stay quiet and follow my lead." The two trolls stood either side of her, holding her by the arms. They stepped forward and pushed open the door.

CHAPTER 28

TWO SPELLS

The din hit us like an explosion as soon as the doors opened. We entered a vast hall packed with Underlanders. Arranged about the space were tables built from large slabs of slate set upon stacked piles of rock. An assortment of weapons lay scattered haphazardly about the place. I counted four rock mantises with metal collars around their necks, chained to the walls, straining to break free and wreak havoc. Many Underlanders were up on the tables, dancing and shouting, while others poured luminous liquid from huge clay jugs into clay tankards, which they then drank with great enthusiasm. There were large clay bowls on the tables, filled with grubs and beetles that the Underlanders scooped up in great handfuls and stuffed into their graveyard mouths. This was a banquet being held on the eve of battle, and the energy emanating throughout the hall was cracking like a brooding lightning storm.

We proceeded down the centre aisle, towards the

table at the far end of the hall. As more and more Underlanders became aware of our presence the noise gradually died down, so that by the time we reached the foot of the steps leading up to Bowelcreep's table, there was total silence.

Wearing its disguise, the largest troll moved forward and stood on the bottom step to address Bowelcreep and his entourage.

"My Lord, we have found trespassers wandering your lands."

There followed a great deal of mumbling and whispering from the throng behind us. Bowelcreep remained seated on his throne, arms folded, his face tightening into a sneer.

"The old one was carrying this," said the larger troll, opening its hand to reveal the Sun Star.

Bowelcreep's eyes widened. He cleared his throat, which sounded like bags of shingle being dropped into a skip.

"Well I never," he said, running his tongue across his lips. "If it isn't the Sun Star. I wonder if the stories are true …"

He leaned forward to take the glass bottle from the troll's hand. He held it up between his thumb and forefinger, eyeing it somewhat suspiciously.

"They say it was blessed in the rays of the first dawn, isn't that right?" he said looking at the Oak Mother. She nodded her head.

"They say its powers are beyond measure. True?"

Again she nodded.

Bowelcreep continued to eye the Sun Star, his tongue still slithering from one side of his mouth to the other. "I must say, it looks rather limp and lifeless." He began shaking the bottle vigorously.

"It is sleeping," said the Oak Mother holding up her hand to make him stop. "It can only be woken by its guardian."

"Let me guess, you are the guardian?" said Bowelcreep still shaking the bottle.

The Oak Mother gently nodded her head. With a gnarled finger, Bowelcreep beckoned the Oak Mother to move closer. The Oak Mother walked up the few steps until she was stood in front of him, her face level with his knees.

"You will waken the flower and hand its power over to me," he said.

"No, I will not," replied the Oak Mother, staring fixedly at her enemy. A collective gasp echoed around the room. Bowelcreep let out a deep sigh before signalling to the guards either side of him with a wave of his arm. The guards instantly moved towards the Oak Mother until the points of their spears were pressed against her clothing.

"I'll say this once more old woman," hissed Bowelcreep. "You will waken the flower and hand its power over to me."

The Oak Mother looked back over her shoulder at us, a forlorn expression on her face. She turned her head away and took a piece of paper from a pocket inside her coat.

"What is that?" said Bowelcreep.

"This is the incantation that will waken the Sun Star. I must ask for complete silence as I speak the words," said the Oak Mother, her voice sounding small and timid.

"Very well, just get on with it," said Bowelcreep.

I felt Aislinn's fingers grip mine. I turned my head just enough to see her look at me before she shut her eyes. I gave the faintest of nods and gently reached for the Old Green Grumble's hand. He twitched slightly and looked at me, surprised. Then as he saw me bow my head and close my eyes, he followed my actions. I felt the ripple as one by one the message got passed by touch along the row until we had all closed our eyes and bowed our heads.

The Oak Mother began to speak, in a language as old as the weather. As she did so, the Sun Star's marble white petals began to slowly open up, revealing the flower's radiant gold centre.

"Aww, isn't it paarittee," snarled Bowelcreep mockingly, causing the Underlanders to giggle among themselves. The Oak Mother raised her hand gently, to silence them.

"Pardon me," sneered Bowelcreep and he stared back down at the bottle, from which came swathes of lilac and pale green light.

"What's it doing?" he snapped.

"It's just warming up," said the Oak Mother and she held the Sun Star at arm's length, where it could be seen by every Underlander.

The light spread up and out, filling the entire space with a serene radiance. It was not bright enough to trouble the Underlanders, just enough to hold them mesmerised. The ceiling of the hall was now fizzing with pinpricks of static, which then glowed like the embers of a bonfire. The Underlanders stood staring up, watching as the light formed softly glowing pools before disappearing into the ceiling. The room fell once more into semi-darkness. Aislinn squeezed my fingers. We were now safe to open our eyes.

In silence the Oak Mother took a piece of paper from her coat and placed it in Bowelcreep's hand.

"You will now recite the words you see in front of you." said the Oak Mother and without hesitation, Bowelcreep read the words from the piece of paper.

The Sun Star began to glow again, this time in a series of pulses, like morse code being spelled out in lights. The pulses became more rapid until the room was filled with golden light. The floor below us seemed to disappear, as if we were suspended within a sea of warm amber. Then the light gradually disappeared into the ceiling, the walls and the floor and I felt my whole body slump slightly, as if I'd been held up all this time by the light itself.

Bowelcreep was standing perfectly still, his gaze still fixed on the Sun Star which had now stopped glowing.

"You will let us return to our home," said the Oak Mother – and took the bottle right out of his hand!

She turned back to us and, holding the Sun Star out in front of her, spoke calmly. "Come my friends, let us go home." We followed her without question as she began leading us back down the central aisle. We looked around us in amazement as the Underlanders stood almost frozen to the spot, gazing into space, eyes wide open, mouths agape. Not one of them even twitched as we quietly sauntered out of the hall.

We found ourselves once more in the antechamber. The Oak Mother was looking at the bottle, shaking her head. The Sun Star lay limply inside, its glow completely diminished. Any colour had drained from the petals and the flower's centre, and the leaves and stem were withered and grey.

"Has it died?" I asked tentatively.

"There may still be a chance to save it, if we can get back out into the daylight in time."

"Assuming the daylight has returned," added Rat Kid.

"Have faith, young lady," replied the Oak Mother, as she took out her bag of coins and started rattling them. Almost instantly, the Blue Caps appeared from various crevices and fissures. They headed directly to the Oak Mother, who held out another batch of coins, which the Blue Caps greedily grabbed and snatched from her. We stood at the door made of roots and flint, and the trolls lifted the heavy wooden bar that was holding it shut. The door slowly swung open and the Blue Caps lead us on in total silence.

CHAPTER 29

A WRONG TURN

In a state of bemusement, we made our way back through the tunnels and caverns of the Underlands. Every now and again we would stumble across something of interest that we seemed to have missed on our journey here – an underground forest of luminescent toadstools; a garden of multi-coloured crystals; and a bubbling pool, filled by the water that cascaded down from an overhang in the rock-face above.

As we continued through the labyrinth, I found myself repeatedly humming a tune which, at first, I couldn't identify. After a few maddening minutes of repeating the tune over and over again, something clicked and I started singing the words to the song that Grandad would often play to me on his gramophone.

I'm not a bat or a rat or a cat,
I'm not a gnu or a kangaroo,
I'm not a goose or a moose on the loose,
I am a mole and I live in a hole

I could hear the others chuckling among themselves and some of them began humming the tune along with me. They particularly enjoyed how I sang the last line in a deep voice, as I heard it on the record.

*I'm not a cow or a chow or a sow,
I'm not a snake or a hake or a drake,
I'm not a flea or a wee chimpanzee,
I am a mole and I live in a hole.*

Suddenly, up ahead, where the tunnel turned a corner, I noticed shadows moving across the wall. They grew taller and taller until a group of figures appeared and stood facing us, holding spears and blades.

It was the fierce group of troglodytes, returning to visit our cell, perhaps having decided what they planned to do with us.

We stopped in our tracks and braced ourselves. Each of us knew our luck was wearing thin, as was our resilience. It was then that the Swan Lady began making a series of high-pitched clicks. As she did so, I detected a faint rustling sound coming from the opposite end of the tunnel, steadily growing in volume.

"You'd all better get down on the floor," said the Swan Lady and we followed her lead just as a seething mass of black leathery wings whistled over our hunched bodies and along the passage, hurtling towards the troglodytes. There were shouts and anguished yelps as the torrent of bats flitted and swarmed around the hapless figures, who were forced to drop their weapons and run, waving their arms frantically above their heads, disappearing in all directions. The way ahead was now clear.

"Let's hope we have no more distractions," said the Oak Mother, as she looked forlornly at the Sun Star before putting it back in her pouch. "We must press on. Time is our enemy now."

I did not know how long we had been travelling for. It could have been hours, it could have been days.

What I did know was that I had absolutely no idea where we were. I had not seen any familiar landmarks, nothing that would prompt any recollection of our journey in. I recalled the time I had become separated from my brother and parents while travelling on the London Underground. The panic I felt then, the hopelessness and crushing sense of claustrophobia was returning to me now and I couldn't stop myself from blurting out "We're lost, aren't we."

There was a startled murmur from other members of our group, which grew louder when the Oak Mother admitted, "I'm sorry to say yes, we are lost. All that business with the Troglodytes and the bats has befuddled me and it looks like we've taken a wrong turn somewhere."

"We could be anywhere. We could be stuck down here for days, months even," gasped the Swan Lady. "My birds will all be long dead by the time we get out."

"If we ever do get out!" added the Pig Man.

"S'not so bad down 'ere," said the Old Green Grumble. "Nice an' dark an' dingy, jus' like my shed."

"My mum and dad will be so worried. I feel terrible, what if they think I've run away or been kidnapped or something?" I said, biting my nails and fidgeting from one foot to the other.

"Quiet," said Rat Kid, "I hear something." Once again she twitched her ears, moving them backwards and forwards, sideways and around, to best catch the sound that none of the rest of us could hear.

"It's coming from up ahead," she said and we followed as she moved swiftly along the tunnel.

We came to a crossroads and turned left, as directed by Rat Kid. After a hundred yards or so we came to where a small group of creatures were involved in what appeared to be some kind of construction work. They were barefooted and stood on short furry legs. Their bodies, arms and legs were covered in silky smooth fur while their hands, feet and faces were dusky pink. They moved with great urgency, scooping up earth and stones with their clawed hands and using it to fill in the mouth of one of the tunnels. They were so occupied with their work, they hadn't noticed us approaching them, and they jumped as one when the Oak Mother spoke.

"Sorry to disturb you when you are clearly very busy, but I wonder if you know a quick way out to the Toplands?"

The mole folk twitched their noses and whiskers as they grouped together to discuss the Oak Mother's request among themselves. One of the mole folk stepped forward and took out a large folded map from the knapsack slung over its shoulder. The map was then spread out on the floor. The Oak Mother gestured for the Blue Caps to stand closer to the map and in the blue light we were able to see the sprawling mass of marks and lines. Once opened out fully, the map was the size of my bedsheet. It had been divided into quarters, each section containing a separate map.

"Why are there four different maps?" I asked, my eyes now beginning to cross from staring at the confusion of marks.

"The Underlands are made up of four main layers you see." He pointed to the bottom right quarter of the map. "This section here is the lowest level, where you have all them scuttlenuts, slinkyfeets and crusty-lugs. Delicious. Then, we move up to the second level, which is where we are now. Just about here," he said, jabbing his claw at a point somewhere amidst the network of lines and squiggles that made up the upper right section of the map. "Every tunnel, passageway, contour and landmark is on this map. It's taken us a couple a' hundred seasons to collect this information. This is the only complete map of the Underlands that we know of."

"My friend, I don't wish to sound impatient, but we are running out of time. If you could just let us know which would be the quickest route back to the Otherlands, please," said the Oak Mother.

Once again, the mole folk became engaged in serious debate, involving much pointing to various parts of the map, and tracing possible routes with the tips of their claws. Heads were scratched and chins were stroked, and it made me think of some old black and white film, set in a war room, with officials standing over a huge table, smoking pipes while they moved models of warships and soldiers about.

I could see the Oak Mother anxiously staring at the Sun Star, knowing how costly every further minute spent down here might prove to be.

Finally, the leader folded up the map and put it back in its knapsack. It pointed to the tunnel to the left of us urged us to follow as it started walking. They moved surprisingly quickly and my aching bones protested as I forced myself to keep up with the pace.

Soon we came to a doorway that looked to have been carved into the tunnel wall. The mole showed us into a rectangular chamber, not much bigger than a telephone box. Seven of us managed to squeeze into the chamber, packed like sardines in a tin. I noticed that the floor was made of thick wooden slats, as were the walls and ceiling.

I realised we were standing inside a large wooden crate which creaked and swayed slightly every time one of us moved. The trolls stood outside the entrance, shrugging their shoulders and shaking their heads.

"No room," snapped the mole. "You'll have to go the long way. Turn left, go down there, turn right, turn left again. Actually, you'll never find it, so I'll show you."

"I'm so sorry," said the Oak Mother. "You will have to make your own way back to the top. Once you are there, come find us in the garden and we will celebrate together."

I caught Aislinn's eye and she offered a hopeful smile. Once the mole had made sure we were standing back from the opening, causing even more of a crush in such confinement, it turned its attention to a metal wheel that was set into the outer wall. The mole demonstrated how to turn the wheel to one of the trolls and before long we heard the sound of mechanical clanking and straining wood come from above our heads. There was a short jolt as the crate started moving upwards, and we had only a few seconds to wave goodbye to the trolls and the mole as we disappeared up the lift shaft.

It was exhausting balancing in the rocking lift. Standing upright became a real challenge as the tiredness in my body threatened to overwhelm me. But being so tightly packed with the others, I found I was able to lift my feet, and hang suspended off the floor, wedged between the shoulders of the Pig Man and the Old Green Grumble. It offered some relief, though my stomach was churning slightly from the constant upwards motion. The Oak Mother began to sing quietly to herself.

There is no purer light
Than that which shines
When friends are near,
A beacon burning bright,
When darkness fills the heart with fear

The others began to join in:

A light that shimmers
At our side
Where 'ere we dare to roam
And charges through
Our every thought
As we are called back home.

I closed my eyes. Their voices trailed into silence as I drifted into a shallow slumber. I had no idea how much time had passed before the lift began to slow. With a crunching of gears it ground to a halt. There was the sensation of cold air at our backs and we each shuffled around to face the open side of the lift. We looked out into a domed space like an atrium, on the far side of which was a wooden staircase. The steps led up to an opening in the ceiling of the cave, through which shafts of light came pouring down, casting dappled patterns across the wall and on to the floor.

We walked the short distance across the atrium, and with a final surge of energy, we climbed the stairs.

CHAPTER 30

THE RETURN

There were gasps and cries as we pushed through the tree roots and ivy that half-covered the tunnel opening. We spilled out into the light of day and clean air hit us as if from a blast of dynamite. It took several minutes of squinting, blinking, coughing and gasping before we managed to stand up and take a look around us.

We were on top of the embankment, looking down onto the allotments and the river, where it flowed into the culvert. On the other side of the river, the meadow lay basking in the sun's glow. Bees bumbled and butterflies fluttered as the birds offered their backwards melodies up into the glorious blue above.

The Swan Lady was holding her arms up to the sky, her eyes wide open, her mouth forming the words 'thank you' over and over again. The Lonely Clown started to dance a jig, circling around her and soon the two friends had locked arms, whooping and cheering as they spun each other around. Rat Kid took the Pig Man by his sleeve and dragged him towards the dancing pair.

The four of them joined hands and began hopping and skipping in a circle, getting faster and faster. The Old Green Grumble was kicking up his long gangly legs like Caractacus Potts dancing to *Me Ol' Bamboo*.

The celebrations came to a chaotic end with everyone toppling over and landing in a tangled heap on the ground. Even the Old Green Grumble was laughing hysterically at this point.

Just then, I felt a hand on my shoulder. It was Aislinn pushing past me in a hurry and there was a look of great concern on her face. I followed her over to where the Oak Mother was lying down in the shade of a willow tree. Aislinn knelt down beside her and stroked her wavy white hair.

"Dearest Oak Mother, what is wrong, please tell me," said Aislinn, trying to hide the note of panic in her voice.

"I am very tired," replied the Oak Mother, her eyes fighting to stay open. By now, the others had become aware of the situation and gathered around in silence, passing worried looks between each other. "Such a long journey," she sighed, "and such foolish creatures those Underlanders."

"What did you do to them?" I said, kneeling down beside her. "How come they just let us walk away like that?"

"Firstly, when they ordered me to demonstrate the Sun Star's powers, I did just that. I used its light to cast a distraction spell. Anyone caught looking at the light was instantly held under the spell, hypnotised and totally helpless."

"So that's why you got us to close our eyes?" I said.

"Exactly and once the first spell had taken hold, I knew Bowelcreep would do whatever I asked him to do."

"So you got him to read out the second spell? What was it?" I asked, holding her small hand in mine.

"A reversal spell," said the Oak Mother, her mouth forming a wry smile. "The one that would reverse his own curse."

"You saved us," said Aislinn, "every single one of us."

"I knew that fool would take the bait," chuckled the Oak Mother. "The desire for power has always been his weakness." For a second her face beamed with mischief.

The rest of us sat in silence as we took in what had happened, how simple her plan, how clever she was, how brave she had been.

"S'pose we ought be grateful or summat," grumbled the Old Green Grumble.

"Just as grateful as I am to all of you, for going into that terrible place, and putting your trust in someone like me, an old woman no taller than a tree stump."

"Come on," said Aislinn, "we must get you home."

"I'm staying right here," said the Oak Mother, reaching for her pocket. She held out her hand and there lying limply in its glass container, was the Sun Star. "I want you to look after my books. They're yours now, I know you will make good use of them. And you must take great care of this," said the Oak Mother as she placed the bottle in Aislinn's hand.

"Where are you going?" I asked.

"Oh, that's for me to find out," replied the Oak Mother. "I only hope it's half as wonderful as it is right here." She looked up through the branches of the willow tree and her eyes followed the path of a group of white clouds as they drifted across the sky.

"You truly are a marvel," said Aislinn.

"Maybe we're all a bit marvellous," said the Oak Mother, and she closed her eyes for the very last time.

CHAPTER 31

BIG SCHOOL

It was September, that time of year when the air hits the back of the throat a little harder and the light is sharp, as if summer's wide lazy glow has thinned to a glassy sheen. I stood with Michael, waiting for the school bus, new shoes pinching my toes and the teflon coating of my trousers itchy against my thighs. This was our first year of secondary school.

"Did you hear about that bloke who solved the Masquerade puzzle?" said Michael.

"What about him?" I replied.

"Turns out, he just guessed where the amulet was buried."

"No way."

"Yes way. Apparently, he knows someone who knows the author, and that person gave him a bit of insider information."

"Will he go to prison?"

"Doubt it, it's not like he murdered somebody."

"No, but it's still cheating."

"Well in that case, Mental Jensen should be locked up too. He's always cheating on his homework. I heard he gets Wolfie Smallwood to give him the answers or else he duffs him up."

"Poor Wolfie, he always gets picked on." I began fiddling with the knot of my school tie, which I'd done up too tightly, when the bus rolled into view. Michael and I, along with all the other kids, hitched our bags over our shoulders and shuffled into some sort of queue.

"Alright lads!" came Hewett's voice, as he pushed his way through the line, to join us at the front.

"Get to the back Fatty!" yelled someone. "Yeah, we've been queueing for ages," yelled another.

"I bagsied my place in the queue," he shouted back at them, "didn't I lads?"

"Yeah, sorry everyone, he definitely bagsied it." There was a bit of shoving and swearing as we stepped up onto the bus and made our way to the back seats.

We plonked ourselves down on the seats and unzipped our coats. Michael immediately slid down off the seat and sat hunched on the floor. I looked up and saw that Mental Jensen had come on to the bus and was arguing with the driver, saying he'd been short-changed. Michael was in trouble with Jensen after he'd refused to hand over his lunch money when Jensen had demanded it a couple of days ago. Michael knew there was nowhere to run this time, so the best he could do for now was hide.

Hewett had already opened his *Empire Strikes Back*

lunch box and was eating his sandwiches. I discreetly took a folded note from the pocket of my Parka. I looked down at the note, and read the message, elegantly written in Christmas tree green ink.

We need to start preparations for the Autumn Festival. Shall we meet at the cave after school?

Aislinn

I slipped the note back into my coat pocket and pulled my rucksack on to my lap. I rummaged around inside and took out my maths homework book. I opened it at the empty page that should have been completed last night and started scribbling down answers, my pen jumping and sliding across the page as the bus rattled up to the school gates. Nick looked at me and laughed.

"Good luck," he said.

"I know, teacher's going to kill me!"

"I just hope you've got a good excuse," said Hewett, and I desperately tried to think of one.

The bus wheezed and choked as it pulled up at the stop and I resigned myself to the fact that I would have to spend morning break finishing my homework. I stuffed the book back into my bag and joined my friends, chattering and shouting as we piled out of the bus and dispersed towards our classrooms, about to discover what a new day had in store.

ACKNOWLEDGEMENTS

My childhood memories of growing up in Cirencester in the 1970s have never left me. I'm forever trying to tap in to the feelings of wonder, adventure, magic and danger I'd experienced then; all that boundless imagination and the constant search for the next great thrill. As I turned 50, I felt it was time to somehow record and convey those memories and feelings. As a child I was very much at the mercy of my imagination and the feelings that I describe in the book were very real. In writing this story, I wanted to understand where that fear of the unknown had come from, why as children we are afraid of the dark and why certain places hold a sense of mystery and foreboding.

Most of the locations featured in the book are real locations which as kids we would visit and explore almost everyday. They are still there today, the pig sheds, the culvert, the railway arch and the mill house. We would walk past these on our way to school every morning and try to scare each other, talking about the clown that lived in the copse, or the pig man that lived in the big grey house. There were playground rumours about the giant rat that lived in the culvert and grandparents seemed to delight in telling stories to their grandchildren about the ghost that haunted the Golden Farm pub. As a child, my imagination often got the better of me and I would be convinced that I was going to encounter one of these beings at some point.

This story definitely started as a memoir and soon became a way of paying tribute to family members and friends that are no longer with me. My beloved brother, Nick passed away in 2017 at the age of 47 and I lost my dear friend Nick Hewett in 1997, at the age of 25. (Hewett's first name is also Nicholas, but we always called him by his surname to differentiate from my brother.) Mum and Dad and my grandparents have all now passed on and writing the book has allowed me to remember them and what they mean to me.

I'd always wanted to write a children's book. As soon as I started writing about my adventures in City Bank and along the old railway line, the characters presented themselves. They'd always been there.

I would like to thank Paul Skuse, curator of *Cirencester, A Local Town For Local People* Facebook group and Robert Heaven and Derek King (RIP) for their tireless work on the *Old Ciren* Facebook group.

These resources have proved invaluable to me in researching local traditions, events, memories and archive images. The people of Cirencester who have responded to my questions and queries in these groups have provided essential insights and the conversations and interactions have been utterly fascinating.

Thanks also to Lorna Brookes, my editor at Crumps Barn Studio, for her patience, expertise and creativity.

Love to my sister-in-law Tara and my nephew Jude.

And finally, thank you to my wife, Marie-Louise and my son Michael for your endless love and support.

You are everything to me.

ABOUT THE AUTHOR

Steve Skinley is a musician and illustrator. His compositions have appeared in dance, theatre and film productions, and he performs with his wife as vintage song and dance duo *The Mary Lou Revue*.

He lives with his wife, son and their dog Ethel in the Cotswolds.

If you loved this book, you'll love our other great fiction titles ...

Crumps Barn Studio
www.crumpsbarn.online